AN UNEXPECTED MISFORTUNE

BLYTHE BAKER

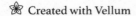 Created with Vellum

Anna's resolution to delve further into the death of her father is interrupted by a fresh murder investigation. When a dinner party at the home of the attractive Jerome Townson ends in violence, it is up to Anna to get to the truth.

But with even her own employer a suspect, will Anna uncover a darker secret than she bargained for, one that could change her life forever?

1

There was a bite in the air that I had not felt in some time, pricking the skin of my cheeks and the tip of my nose. I pulled my scarf up to protect as much of my exposed face as I could.

A scent in the air filled my mind with nostalgia— the swirling smoke pouring from every chimney and the exhaust rumbling from the pipes of the cars that passed me by on the streets.

At once, I was seven years old again, following Sister Mary in a long line of other children. The sidewalk was slick with frost, the fluttering snowflakes dancing in the light from the lampposts. It was a rare snowfall in London, the clouds lying thick overhead, the sounds of blaring horns and shouts of newspaper boys filling the air.

That had been an exciting day. Not only had Sister Mary taken us to the most wonderful of plays at the local theater but then she had guided us all to a bakery owned by her cousin. The sweet, delicate, buttery pastries still filled my mind with brightness, one of the happiest days of my childhood, even if I could only remember bits and pieces, like the feel of the dress I'd worn or the scent of cinnamon before I had taken a bite of my treat.

I smiled, though this day was only partially like that memory. The sky overhead, as grey as on that other occasion so many years before, promised snow. It certainly was cold enough for it, as my breath left my mouth in white, billowy clouds.

I stood on the corner just a few blocks from the orphanage, staring around. The store on the southern corner of the street had once been a florist shop and had since become a department store, having bought the three spaces beside it. The grocer directly across the street from me had changed its name. Thankfully, the toy shop that I used to pass by with my father still remained, with the painted letters on the front window having faded, the display within still displaying its Christmas offerings, the tinsel glittering in the daylight.

Despite the many years I had lived in this area, it did not feel particularly like home. Even when I was young, it always felt like a temporary roost, one that I would finally fly away from. I knew it was never meant to be the place I would remain forever.

I glanced up at the road sign and read the name of the avenue written in green, pointing down the street to my left.

This street, some might say, should be special to me. It was where I had spent the early years of my life, after all.

My heart skipped and a lump appeared in my throat.

I asked myself the same question that I had ten minutes before...should I go down there? Should I open myself up to that sort of discomfort?

I have come this far, I thought, steeling myself. *I can take a peek. It might be some time before I get another chance.*

I started down the street, keeping my gloved hands tucked beneath my arms, hugging myself tightly to preserve as much heat as possible.

The long row of houses had not changed in many years. My father had painted the window frames of ours, telling me even as a young girl that it was one thing my mother had requested every spring. It made our home stand out a bit from the others along the row.

Number 493. The second to last at the end of the road.

I stood on the opposite side of the street. Despite

my longing to go and see it up close, I knew that it no longer belonged to my family. In fact, there were several changes even on first glance that assured me it was very much the home of others now.

Window boxes hung out of the upper windows, and while empty right now, were all painted bright red and white. Curtains hung closed in the large front window, while my father had never drawn ours. A small green wagon sat on the front porch with a stuffed bear resting inside.

Another family is living their lives there, I thought.

For a brief moment, a sharp, quick jab of jealousy pierced my heart. How was it fair that they were able to live out the sort of life I wanted? That was where I should have been, with my mother and father, not having been robbed of what should have been my childhood. I should have had a mother who survived childbirth. I should have grown up with a father who had not met a terrible fate only a few short years later.

I tugged on the reins of my emotions. Bitterness would achieve nothing.

I turned and started back down the street, away from the house and away from the memories that weighed heavy upon me.

I stopped at the corner, the house out of sight, and breathed a bit easier.

I should have known better.

I rubbed my hands up and down my arms, feeling

strange. Seeing the home robbed me of the nostalgia that I had carried around with me for years. The details had faded with time. After awhile, all I had seen was the ideal picture of it. Before today, I had not remembered the cracks in the bricks of the stairs or the crack in the top right window. Had those happened when I was there? Or long since?

I was many years removed from when I had lived there. That was a great deal of time for life to happen and for decay to take over. How had I forgotten the smoke stacks in the distance from the end of the road? Or the siren that sang two streets over from the fire station?

Some of the romance of the place had been stripped away.

I should have left it as it was in my mind, I thought. No longer could I think on it so fondly.

Feeling worse than I had before, I started down the street toward my true destination, the reason I had come to the opposite side of London from Mrs. Montford's home.

Walking the streets of my childhood made me feel like I was walking through a storybook of someone else's life.

I have become an entirely different person in the time since I last lived here, I thought.

I passed by a bakery, seeing freshly baked loaves tucked in woven baskets in the window, the warm scent of yeast trickling through the door. I stopped and caught sight of my reflection.

That is not entirely true, is it? What changed me wasn't time but events, the events that happened to that little girl I used to be, when she witnessed something no child should ever have to.

I had been running from that memory my whole life, and in the past two months, the shadows had finally caught up with me. Death had become far too frequent a visitor to ignore, of late.

The breads in the window no longer looked appetizing. I continued on my way.

I turned a corner and the orphanage appeared. It nestled along the outside of a roundabout, with a small circular green in the center with a statue of some important general from many, many years ago. The building stood next to a church on one side and a row of homes on the other.

It looked just as I remembered, with the same slotted shutters, the thick, lead panes in the windows, and made of the same orange brick. The only difference was that the last time I had seen it, the small tree planted out front had been in full spring bloom and the sky had been bright, brilliant blue instead of the dull, ashen grey it was today.

I hesitated. I did not expect much of a homecoming, but at the same time, I knew my return would not go unnoticed. Many people, both the Sisters and the older children, would likely remember me from my time there. It had only been four years since I had left, after all.

I had a mission, though, and could not be put off by a dread of staring old memories in the face. I had come all the way out here, to this side of the city, to find out some very important information.

I needed to know more about my past and the only way to learn what I needed was to step back into a part of it, as difficult as that might be.

I started around the street, keeping my eye on the orphanage at the far end. Cars followed after one another on the roundabout, a few horns blaring, the hum of engines filling the air. The smoke from the smokestacks on the factory at the edge of the river, no more than a mile or two away, billowed up to meet and meld with the clouds.

The best way for me to overcome my nervousness about the whole matter was to simply face it head on.

What would everyone say when they saw me? Would they be happy to see me? Would I be happy to see them?

I had mixed feelings on how I thought of my upbringing at the orphanage. It had not been bad but it had not been all good, either.

I stopped a short distance from the steps leading up to the front door. I glanced up at the windows, at the top floor, the second window from the right—my old bedroom that I had shared with several other girls my age. We had a view of the roundabout and the stretch of green. A view I had seen every day for the majority of my life.

Still, it felt like a distant dream.

I mustered my courage and started toward the door.

The answers I need are here, I thought. *And I need to find them if I ever hope to learn the truth.*

I LAID my hand on the brass knocker on the door, my heart sinking. *I have never done this before,* I thought. *Not here, at least.*

At a place that had been my home, I had never come as a guest. It felt bizarre as I lifted the cold metal, knocking it three times against the plate beneath it, and letting it fall back down.

Why did I feel so strange being here? Why did I feel so exposed and vulnerable?

I did not appreciate the feeling and hoped that once the tension of setting foot inside had come and passed, it would ease the frantic beating of my heart.

Footsteps, muffled through the door, were first to greet me before it was pulled open.

The familiar green eyes of Sister Mary fell upon me and quickly widened with recognition. "Anna?" she asked, her smile growing, forming wrinkles that had not existed the last time I had seen her. "My heavens, it is you, isn't it? What are you doing back here?"

I smiled in return, the knots in my stomach easing a little. "I thought I would come for a visit," I said.

"Well, come in, come in," she said, stepping aside, waving me in. "Get out of that cold."

I followed her in, and the familiar smell of books, leather, and aged wood washed over me, making me feel as if I were a child again.

"Here, allow me to take your coat," Sister Mary said, closing the door behind me. "You *must* stay for tea. I insist."

"That would be lovely, thank you," I said, allowing her to take my coat and scarf.

She looked up into my face, her own round one glowing with happiness. "It is so good to see you, dear," she said. She started toward the parlor, which was just off the open room that was used for school.

"Come sit down," she said, offering me the green velvet seat near the large front window.

"Thank you," I said, easing myself into the chair.

"Just let me go and fetch a few of the children who will remember you," Sister Mary said brightly. "Several of the younger ones you used to help care for are older now, but still with us."

I said, "Actually, I was hoping to see..."

But I had no opportunity to explain the true reason

for my visit, because she was already halfway to the door.

"The children will be delighted to see a familiar visitor," she called back over her shoulder, before she disappeared around the corner.

I sat there rigidly, wondering if I had made a mistake in coming here. What if I never found the chance to state my true business?

"Well...you were not who I expected to see."

I jumped at the sound of that voice and whipped around to see Sister Nancy stride through the side door of the room, her expression as stern as it ever was. "I saw Sister Mary in the hall. She said we had a guest."

My face flooded with color, although I had no particular reason to feel guilty. It was not as if I had lied about my purpose in being here. Not exactly. There was nothing wrong in it.

"Yes, ma'am," I said, clutching the small handbag I had brought with me to my middle. "How do you do?"

Sister Nancy stopped a short distance away and folded her arms. I noticed that she, like Sister Mary, had aged slightly with the years.

"I am fine, thank you," she said. "What brings you all the way back to London? I assume you are in need of something?"

I opened my mouth to answer when the sound of excited shrieks echoed down from the floor above. Not a moment later, the sound of thunderous footsteps on the stairs signaled the imminent arrival of the children.

I barely had time to rise to my feet before six cheery faces burst into the room and paused only for a moment as we recognized one another. The children all raced, one after the other, throwing themselves at me.

My pleasure at seeing them was unexpectedly genuine, but I scrambled to remember all of their names.

"Molly! Richard!" I said, doing my best not to fall beneath the profound weight of them all piling against me. "Oh, Tilly, do not worry, I see you, too! Hello, Bernard. And Emily! My, look how much you have all grown!"

We shared a few more moments of speaking over one another, excitedly exchanging greetings.

"We had no idea you would be coming," said a young girl with chestnut hair, clasping her hands tightly in front of herself, her shoulders quivering in excitement.

She must have stood a whole foot taller than when I had last seen her. "Emily..." I said. "Look how tall you are."

"I'm ten now," she said, swishing her skirts bashfully.

"We received your letter for Christmas," said the older girl standing behind her.

I looked into the pretty face of Molly, who still harbored some childhood freckles on her cheeks, her dark hair cut much the same way my own was, bobbed just below the ears. She must have been almost sixteen, now.

"Did you?" I asked. "Oh, that is good. I hope it did not arrive too late."

"Three days before," said Molly, and her face split into a smile.

"Have you come all this way just to say hello?" asked the boy standing beside Sister Mary.

I returned his smile. "Well, Richard, my visit was for two purposes," I said. "To say hello to you all, of course."

I looked over at Sister Mary, knowing I would never get a better opportunity than this. "I also hoped to speak with Sister Margaret, if she would see me."

A hush fell over the room.

"Sister Margaret...has been quite busy of late," Sister Mary said. "The funding has gone down, you see, and she has been making some very difficult decisions about how to keep everything running smoothly."

"I'm sorry," I said. "I did not realize that my timing was so poor."

Sister Mary nodded. "One of the great benefactors of our orphanage has recently passed away and his son had no interest in continuing to send us a monthly stipend. That being the case, Sister Margaret has been quite frantic and not in the best of moods."

"Do you think she will not see me, then?" I asked, my heart picking up its pace.

Sister Mary frowned. "I do not know," she said. "I will go and speak with her."

"Thank you," I said. "I do appreciate it."

Sister Mary nodded and left the room. Sister Nancy, I now realized, had already slipped away, as well.

I spent the next few anxious moments talking with the children, asking after them and what had happened in the few years that I had been gone. It seemed the orphanage had adopted a cat, who lived in the girls' room. Tilly had learned how to play the piano and led everyone in caroling on Christmas Eve. Bernard had made it his goal to read every book in the library and complained that he was almost halfway through already, wishing he had more to choose from.

I found myself caught up in the excitement of it all when Sister Mary returned to the drawing room.

She shook her head. "Sister Margaret has asked me to send her regards but she cannot spare the time to see you," she said in a nervous tone.

I blinked at her. "What? Why?"

"It is as I said," she answered with a shrug. "She cannot spare the time. She is far too busy."

I pursed my lips. I was not going to have come all

this way simply to be turned around before I had the answers I sought.

"Sister Mary," I said, "would you be so kind as to go and speak with her once more? And please, would you tell her that I have some questions for her about my father?"

"Your...father?"

"Yes," I said. "I would not be so discourteous if I had anywhere else to turn, however, she is the only one who has the information I am after. And I must speak with her."

Sister Mary's expression hardened. "Very well," she said. "I will try once more."

In her absence, the children and I chatted with one another again, briefly.

I was grateful when she returned, a look of determination on her face.

"She will see you," Sister Mary said. "But only for ten minutes."

Ten minutes. In such a short amount of time, I might finally have the answers to questions that had haunted me all these years.

2

I climbed the stairway that I had traversed thousands of times as a child. It was hardly any different now, with several other orphans trailing behind me, whispering to one another, one yelping in pain as another stepped on his toes. The same stair creaked, the third from the top, and without thinking, I put as little of my weight upon it as possible, just as I used to in order not to wake the little ones.

The same green rug ran down the length of the hallway, though it seemed a great deal more tattered and faded than I remembered it.

Young Emily tugged on the sides of my skirt. "Anna, will you come see my dolly after you see Sister Margaret?" she asked.

"If I have time," I said, nodding down to her. "Now, run along."

"Make sure you come say goodbye before you leave," Richard said, ushering the other children away.

"Of course," I said.

As the children hurried back down to a lower landing, Sister Mary drew my attention to the doorway we had reached. "Sister Margaret will be none too happy if you keep her waiting."

"Right," I said.

She nodded at me and then walked back to the stairs, heading down, leaving me alone to face Sister Margaret's office.

I could count how many times I had been behind this door on one hand. The first had been when I had fallen and skinned my knee while playing out in the courtyard. The shock of being sent all the way up here had pained me more than the wound, but I had nothing more than a bandage to tell of afterward. The second time, some years later, had been when another girl had accused me of stealing her locket. She had carried on and on for so long that Sister Mary had eventually dragged us up here together so that Sister Margaret could sort us out.

The few other times had been to ask for help in slight emergencies with the other children, but every time had filled me with the same dread as I felt now.

Do not be so foolish, I scolded myself. *Sister Margaret has no authority in your life now. You have nothing to worry about.*

I straightened my shoulders, though my palms were clammy, and raised my hand to knock at the door.

"Anna, is that you?" came Sister Margaret's muffled voice.

"Yes, Sister," I said, my heart lodged in my throat.

"Well, do not keep me waiting," she said.

I did as she asked and walked inside.

Her study had changed very little since I had last stepped within. The globe still sat beneath the window, the same walnut desk right in front of it. Shelves flanked both sides, though only a select number of books had been neatly arranged upon it.

Sister Margaret sat at the desk wearing the same black dress as the other Sisters. Bent over a piece of paper, she scribbled away with a pen in her nearly ineligible writing. A stack of similar papers stood beside it, along with a pile of blank envelopes, ready for marking.

She glanced up at me as I entered, her dark eyes combing me up and down. "Well, now," she said, sitting up straight, leaning back in her seat. "It is good to see you, Anna."

I smiled at her, the unease in my heart lessening slightly. "It is good to see you as well, Sister Margaret."

"Come in," she said, gesturing to a chair along the wall opposite her desk. "I apologize for the mess but I hardly seem to have the time to clean any of it up."

"It is no trouble," I said, taking one of the seats, feeling a great deal like I was ten years old again.

"And as much as I would like to sit and ask you all about your life, I simply am unable to do so," Sister Margaret said, looking at me down the length of her nose. "I shall address your request only because you have come so far for it. A letter might have been more appropriate but this will certainly be quicker."

My cheeks flushed with emotion. "Well..." I said, watching as she flipped the paper over and continued to write on the other side. "I..."

"Come, girl, I do not have all day," Sister Margaret said with clear exasperation, giving me a flat look. "Sister Mary said you have some questions for me?"

"I do, yes," I said, my fingers knotting in the leather of my small clutch. "About my father, in fact."

Sister Margaret stopped her writing, her eyes fixed to the page. She let out a long, slow exhale through her nose before removing her spectacles and setting them down beside her. "Your father?" she asked. "Why do you imagine I know anything about your father?"

"I...do not know," I said. "When he was killed, I was only six years old. I expect that whoever brought me here might have told you *something*."

Sister Margaret studied me, her eyes as unreadable as they ever were.

"It was a policeman that brought you here," she said. "It was the middle of the night and a terrible storm had blown in. I had only just managed to get one of the babies to sleep in her crib, when there was a frantic knock at the door. A quick explanation told me you had been found at your home, weeping so loudly that your neighbors could hear you."

The memories touched the edges of my mind; a firm hand clutching my own tightly as we hurried down the street, then sitting alone in the dark foyer below, the sound of the thunder overhead...

I blinked. I had not remembered that until now.

"Did the policeman know anything about my father?" I asked.

"When he brought you to us, he said you were entirely alone," she said. "We learned a great deal of what happened from what you told us."

"I was so young," I said. "I could not possibly have made any sense."

"You certainly did not," Sister Margaret said, her eyes narrowing further. "Tell me, why is it that you are so interested in this now? Why did you never ask these sorts of questions when you were living here?"

I hesitated. How much did I want to share with her? Should I mention the Colonel's death and how it had jogged some memories of my past from the far recesses of my mind? It did not seem wise. I did not wish to frighten her and I did not know how much would even be appropriate for me to share. What would Mrs. Montford say if I were to tell everyone the details of her husband's murder?

"I suppose...my past has come to light these last few months," I said, choosing my words carefully. "I want to find out what happened to my father, or if there is anything that you can tell me about my life before I came here to the orphanage."

"My dear, you should know that the information we receive about the children who come to stay with us is often very limited," she said.

I glanced over my shoulder to a long narrow file cabinet along the back wall. "Yes but do you not keep information about the children in there?" I asked. "Copies of the files that you give to the parents when they adopt?"

"I certainly do," Sister Margaret said, getting to her feet. "But I can assure you that your folder is one of the slimmest of them all."

She looked at the clock up on the wall and her expression hardened. She then reached for a stack of books on a chair beside her, filling her arms.

"I am sorry, Anna. As pleased as I am to see the young woman you have grown into, I do have other matters to which I must attend," she said, going to the door and opening it. She stood beside it, looking at me. "You are welcome to stay as long as you would like but I am to be meeting with a possible sponsor for the new year."

I could see that I was no longer wanted. I rose, as well, and made my way to the door. "Of course, Sister," I said. I followed her out into the hall and she promptly pulled the door closed behind her.

"It really was pleasant to see you again," she said. "Do come back and visit the children soon, all right?"

"Thank you, Sister," I said.

With a firm nod, she hurried toward the stairs and started down them without another look back over her shoulder at me.

I lingered there in the hall, hearing her echoing footsteps fading from earshot.

I supposed there was no reason to stay up here, given that she did not share the information I needed.

I hesitated, having taken a small step away, and looked back over my shoulder at the door. It gave me pause that Sister Margaret did not give me a precise answer to my question. I had asked her about my father and she had avoided the subject. Had it been intentional?

That, accompanied with her sudden desire to get up and leave the room, taking me with her, demonstrated that she did have something to hide.

But what?

My heart skipped as I stood there in the middle of the hall. I could move away, leave it as it was, and then I would simply be as uninformed as I had been when I came in.

Or...

The warning bells sounding in my mind reverberated, warning me not to turn and walk back. I would be trespassing, stealing, no better than a thief.

And yet, was this information not my own for knowing? Had I not some right to the truth?

I swallowed, my throat dry.

It would not be long before the others downstairs would wonder where I was, if the person I was supposedly meeting with had come and gone.

They would be expecting me to come downstairs sooner or later. If I was going to act, then I needed to act *now*.

I made up my mind. I could not convince Sister Margaret to provide me the information I wanted or needed. Whether she was intentionally barring me or not did not matter. I had come all this way to find answers and I was not going to be able to come back in search for them for a while again.

I chanced the door knob and found it unlocked. I twisted the handle but my hand could scarcely get a grip due to the sweat making it slick beneath my skin.

I will not linger, I thought, tiptoeing through the empty room to the very file cabinet that I had indicated to Sister Margaret moments before. *I will only need a moment to examine my folder.*

My fingers shook as I reached out for the handle of

the drawer, closing around it. I gave it a tug and was met with a loud *creak*.

I stopped, whipping around to face the door. If Sister Margaret caught me in here, there was no telling what she would do. Could I be reported to the authorities for trespassing to view my own file?

The moments passed and I remained undetected. My heartbeat began to slow. I realized that if she had not come racing back by now, then I was likely in the clear.

My time was short, though, before someone else came looking for me.

I eased the drawer the rest of the way open and was surprised to see the number of folders within. There had to have been over one hundred. Was this how many children had come and gone from the orphanage over the years?

Thankfully, as I started to go through them, I saw that Sister Margaret had organized them by last name, alphabetically. It only took me a few moments to get to *Fairweather*.

I pulled the folder from the drawer and let it fall open atop the stacks of other folders.

Sister Margaret had not been lying when she told me that my folder was thin. Only three pieces of paper lay within, all written in the same elegant hand that I recognized at once as Sister Mary's.

The date scrawled at the top of the first page read *January 8th*, along with a chunk of text.

She was brought to us this evening in the middle of the night by a policeman. He told us that she was found in her home, entirely alone, and was only discovered by her mournful wails heard by neighbors.

My heart clenched within me. I only vaguely remembered this. The time between the moment my father was killed and when I arrived at the orphanage was murky. I could not be certain if it was the distance from that time or the sheer shock on my young mind that had caused me to so readily forget.

The police will speak with the neighbors come morning to discern whether the girl has any living relatives able to keep her. We certainly have the room for her if she has nowhere else to go, but as always, we would prefer her to be with her own family.

I flipped the page over and found a basic list of information about me gathered over the years. It included my date of birth, my full name, and other knowledge that had been gleaned about me.

She is cautious and shy but quite intelligent. She can be utterly trusted to complete any tasks given to her and will do whatever is asked of her with great precision and diligence.

Such an assessment to be made of a young woman was quite possibly the reason Mrs. Montford and the

Colonel had chosen to hire me. What more could one want from a potential servant?

I turned to the last page and found more hand-written notes.

I quickly read through them, my eyes widening the further I read.

The sound of a rather loud *thump* echoed from downstairs, causing me to jump.

I quickly pulled a small pad and pencil from within my clutch purse and scrawled down a few notes of my own, copying as much as I could for as long as I dared do so, before shoving the notebook back inside and hurrying from the room.

3

It was raining by the time I returned to Mrs. Montford's home. Not a pleasant rain that made one think of good books and warm fires but the sleety, icy sort of rain that made the skin of one's face feel as if it were covered in a sheen of frost.

"Good heavens, Miss Fairweather," Mr. Fitzroy said as he helped to peel the sleeves of my drenched coat from my arms. "Why were you out in this horrendous weather?"

"I had a visit to make," I told the butler.

"To see friends?"

"Something like that," I said vaguely.

"And did you have a pleasant trip?" he asked.

"I did." I shivered, even as all my outerwear was set out to dry over the radiators along the wall.

I decided to look in on my mistress. I stepped into

the parlor where Mrs. Montford sat in her usual spot, reading a book that had been sent to her by one of her cousins for Christmas. She did not even look up as I entered.

"Hello, Mrs. Montford," I said, fetching her prepared teapot from the credenza that Mrs. Rose had set out.

She glanced up. "Ah, there you are," she said, returning her eyes to her book. "I hope your outing was agreeable?"

"Yes, thank you," I said.

She turned the page, her eyes still roaming over the words. "I imagine it was quite interesting to see the place again," she said. "How long has it been now?"

"Four years, ma'am," I said, pouring the steaming hot tea into the cup resting beside her. I saw she had selected one of her pink teacups, a set that I had not yet seen since we had arrived in London.

"Goodness me, that long already?" she asked.

I ladled two cubes of sugar into her tea and just the right amount of milk before giving it a good swirl with her spoon. "Indeed, ma'am," I said.

"I am glad that you took my advice, you know," she said.

I stepped back, giving her some space to enjoy her tea. "I am grateful," I said. "You were very kind to give me the morning to go and see them."

"Well, I thought it was time that you took some

time for yourself," she said.

She was not wrong. Every other week, I had Tuesday mornings to myself before noon. I often stayed in my room, enjoying a book or writing letters. It gave me a chance to catch up on anything I might need to do for myself, such as mending a garment or tidying my space. This was different, though. She had sprung the idea on me only three days before, telling me that after all I had been through recently, all the dangers I had endured, I should get away from the house and seek out familiar faces in order to recoup.

I knew it may have been due to the absentminded-ness that I had been fighting. Sleep had been evading me at night, and so, my ability to function properly during the day had been difficult at times. I thought the moment that convinced her to push the idea was when I had poured tea all over the dining room table instead of into her cup and saucer during breakfast.

"You have never asked for extra time," Mrs. Mont-ford went on, after I did not answer her. "That being the case, I knew that you needed a change of pace. Tell me, did it help?"

Did it? I wondered.

I did not know what to say. The memories of the past few weeks had been haunting me and they only seemed to be piling up on top of me. Every time I thought I had managed to get away from it all, another tragedy struck.

"I believe it did help, in a way," I said. "Seeing the faces of some of those children again lifted my spirits considerably."

"I am pleased to hear it," Mrs. Montford said, lifting her tea and blowing on it gently to cool it before taking a sip. She sighed with contentment. "Though I must admit, you were missed this morning, as you are the only one who seems able to get my tea just right."

I tended to Mrs. Montford for the rest of her tea time, wherein we engaged in some light conversation about how I had found the orphanage and whether it had changed since my time there.

I did not, however, tell her what I had learned from Sister Margaret, or of the notes I had scrawled down in the pad I had brought with me. Every time I thought of those few, frantic moments in the dark office, my heart fluttered. How foolish I had been, how easily I could have been discovered. Then what would I have done?

As I went about the rest of our day, helping Mrs. Montford dress for dinner and standing by as she sat at the fireside before bed, my thoughts kept drifting back to those notes. There was a great deal that I had to think over but I did not feel I could, or should, exert the energy needed to do so while trying to attend to my tasks.

It was not until the end of the day that I found my way back to my room.

My friend and fellow servant, Selina, and I had met

briefly in the kitchens before bed. She had told me of the day's events, which had been altogether unexciting, to my relief. It seemed the most interesting thing that had occurred had been when another servant, George, found himself covered in soot after chasing after a bat that had tried to fly up the chimney in the kitchen.

I let out a long, heavy sigh as I heard the latch close behind me and sank against my bedroom door to allow myself a chance to breathe for a moment or two.

This was the moment I had been waiting for all afternoon, the chance to read through what I had discovered that morning once again.

I picked up my clutch that I had laid aside on my writing desk and carried it to the bed. I sank down onto the end and pulled my legs up underneath me, tucking them in.

My heart began to beat more quickly as I tugged open the zipper.

I ran my hand over the notepad, knowing that the truth I had been denied so long lay within and I had not properly had the chance to understand it. Questions had plagued me about it all day. I wanted to see if what I had thought I had read had indeed been the truth.

I hesitated. How would I handle what I found? Would it give me peace? Or simply create more confusion?

This might be the end of my information, I realized.

There may not be any further avenues for me to explore.

I opened the pad and flipped toward the back to where I knew I had written down what I had been able to.

The third page that I had stumbled upon in my file had been where the most information had been kept. It also seemed to be from several different times, as the heaviness of the ink and the nib of the pen chosen to write with seemed to change.

All of them, I had realized, had been written by Sister Mary, who must have been the one to keep the majority of the notes on the children.

Anna Fairweather came to us early in January, her father seemingly having passed away just a few days before and neighbors having discovered the child alone. From speaking with the police, it appears little is known about the man's death. His daughter has been reluctant to give us any information.

I remembered that time. I did not believe I shared anything about my father's death with anyone for some years to come. In my young mind, I feared that if I did, whoever it was that had harmed my father would come for me, as well. I had somehow convinced myself that keeping it a secret was the best way to keep myself safe. Little did I know that I had only been causing myself more harm than good. Perhaps the perpetrator could have been caught, had I had the bravery to speak out back then.

I certainly wished there was a bit more information about my father. Had I been the only one to witness his murder? Would I never know the truth about his untimely demise?

I took a deep breath and continued on.

I remembered the next set of notes looked different and perhaps a bit neater. I assumed she would have had more time to record them.

An interesting discovery has been made at the Fairweather home. The police have brought some items over that might have importance to Anna, both for her future and her present.

I did remember that time. They had asked me if I wanted to accompany the police clearing out the home. Sister Mary had offered to go along with me but I had refused, as I had been too frightened to go into the house again. Instead, they had brought me some things that I had asked for but looked also for anything that might be of importance. It seemed that they had discovered more than I had ever been told of.

There was a will, belonging to the poor girl's father, stating that if anything were to happen to him as it had his wife, care for Anna would fall to one of his two sisters, a one Miss Elizabeth Fairweather, or a Mrs. Rosaline Tempest, formerly Fairweather. They had seemingly agreed upon the time of the signing of the will to take on the responsibility of her care.

With great excitement, we spent nearly a week looking

for the women in question. It was bound to be difficult, as little Anna does not remember them, nor does she seem to have ever met them. Unfortunately, when the authorities were able to find and visit Miss Elizabeth Fairweather, she denied knowledge of any such agreement.

We sent her half a dozen letters over several months but never heard any further response, after her initial refusal to speak further with the authorities.

That was the end of it all. I could not remember if there had been a great deal more but it had been all I had managed to write down before I felt as if I might get caught.

I could not imagine there had been a great deal more but what surprised me most was that I did not remember hearing about these two women, my aunts. I had always known that my father had sisters, as he had spoken of them when I was young. I thought I remembered family members from different social engagements before he had died. I did not think, however, that I could have picked them out of a room full of people, unless they looked a great deal like my father. I only ever could clearly remember his likeness from the small portrait that I had inside the locket that had once belonged to my mother, a gift from before they had married.

Regardless, I realized that Sister Mary had kept the information from me for a reason. Perhaps she did not want to give a young girl any hope of a better life when it had quite clearly never come. Would that have broken my spirit even further? Knowing myself and how I had been so young, I knew that it would have.

I set the notepad aside, feeling somewhat detached. Why had those women chosen to forsake me, even after signing a document alongside my father promising to do the opposite? Did such a binding statement mean so little? Yet, it had happened so long ago. The truth was that learning what I had changed nothing about my current circumstances or the life that I found myself in.

I rose from the bed and strode to the window, staring toward the east, toward where the orphanage and my old home resided. I reached for the shawl draped over the back of my chair and drew it around my shoulders.

My life would likely have been quite different if either of my aunts had chosen to honor their word. But would my position be any better than it was now?

It will not do to think on these matters, especially when nothing can or will change, I thought. It was not possible to go back to that time in my life and somehow find my aunts. *And who knows? Perhaps my life would have been far worse than what it has been. The grass is not always greener, as they say.*

"No..." I muttered underneath my breath. "It is best if I simply set these facts aside and leave them in the past where they belong."

I turned around and grabbed my pad of paper and returned it to the small drawer in the desk.

I knew that I might be able to locate these women now. What would stop me? Of course, it was entirely possible that one or both of them could have passed away by now, and I would have been none the wiser. Still, they were the only two people that I could consider family.

Would you truly wish to speak with them after they rejected you?

I paused, my heart sinking.

I did not know.

The only positive in that thought was that they had been so close to my father, and as such, perhaps they would be able to help me learn the truth about what had happened to him. After he died, that chapter in my life had ended. There would be nowhere else I could turn to find the truth. I had no idea who knew him and who did not. I did not even know if anyone would still recognize the name of Fairweather.

I changed into my night clothes and sank into bed, the cold bedding chilling me to my very core.

How strange life can be...

Perhaps it would not hurt to look for them. If I found them, perhaps they could help me understand who might have killed my father...and why I felt, in my nightmares, as if I recognized the killer.

4

There was only one problem that I could see in all this: I had no idea where to find these two aunts of mine that I had learned of in Sister Margaret's file. I knew at least one of them must have resided in London, given the fact that the authorities had been able to go to her home. I knew nothing about her sister, not even if she had once lived in London or if she did any longer. The task was monumental.

Another problem I realized come the morning was that I did not know whether to voice the problem to Mrs. Montford. Of course, it was something that I could do on my own time but I knew that her connections could prove quite useful, if she were willing to give me the help I asked for.

I debated about it through breakfast. It was not

until I bumped into Selina during Mrs. Montford's midmorning rest that I asked myself if I truly wanted to admit what I had discovered to anyone. If I did, then I would have to admit that I had sneaked a look at the information in the first place. I was not eager to confess my guilt, lest anything bad come of it.

I had little time to think on the matter, however, as Mrs. Montford insisted I accompany her that evening as her companion to the home of her sister-in-law Mrs. Townson for a dinner party to celebrate the new year.

Alone with my employer in the car, I considered sharing my concerns with her but the chance never felt right. She was too busy speaking with our driver about the large tree in the neighborhood square that had been decorated for Christmas, wondering aloud whether it would be taken down just after the new year or if it would be left alone for a while.

We arrived at Mrs. Townson's house, and even from the first glance out the window, I could see that we were not the first to arrive. Two other cars had been parked out in front of the rowhouse that stood just a short distance from the river, a lovely home that was comparable to my mistress's. The brick had been painted in a light grey, which seemed a great deal more pleasing than the bright red that I had seen across the bridge on the way through the city.

I felt nervous as we got out of the car. This was Mrs.

Townson's home, wasn't it? Then the likelihood of my seeing her son Mr. Jerome was quite high.

I wondered if he would try and speak with me that night. It would not be lost on anyone if he were to seek out private conversation with his aunt's maid and companion, which he likely would. It would certainly raise some eyebrows.

We were welcomed in as if Mrs. Montford and Mrs. Townson were dear old friends. The butler of my mistress's sister-in-law was a rather handsome man some years younger than our own Mr. Fitzroy.

"Allow me to take your coats and show you to the drawing room," he offered pleasantly.

"Thank you," Mrs. Montford said, allowing him to pull the coat from her arms.

He took us to the drawing room, a lovely room that had been papered in an emerald green and adorned with walnut tables and red velvet chairs. A smart look, to be sure, but it certainly did seem a great deal bolder than I would have expected from Mrs. Townson. Perhaps it had been to her late husband's taste?

Mrs. Montford was welcomed by a throng of people gathered near the fireplace, which gave me the opportunity to slowly disappear into the shadows along the wall. I would not be much noticed here and would be near enough to serve my mistress if she required me for any errand. It was a relief to slip away and nestle myself in beside the paintings and the small bronze statue of a lion that rested on top of a table beside me. It gleamed in the light of the candles nearby, having obviously been recently polished.

I settled into one of the velvet armchairs, happy to have finally arrived, knowing that the rest of the night would be nothing more than simple frivolity, laughter, and almost certainly good food.

Christmas may have been over but it seemed that Mrs. Townson wanted to leave a few reminders dotted about the room in the form of a garland hanging from the fireplace mantle, as well as the many candles that had been wrapped in strands of berries. The quiet, slow time between Christmas and the new year always seemed to blur together in my mind but never in a bad way. Instead, whenever I thought of this time in years past, it always filled my heart with warmth, comfort, and the simple enjoyments of a quiet life.

It seemed the other guests had pleasant times with their families during Christmas as well. All shared stories with one another in excited, happy tones. It pleased me to see Mrs. Montford smiling as much as she was. She even surprised me a little when she made her way to greet Mrs. Townson herself. A seemingly polite conversation followed, as if the two had not been enemies until recently.

My eyes passed over the room. I did not find Mr. Jerome anywhere and I wondered if he was in attendance.

At that moment, I saw an unfamiliar man extricate himself from the group he had been speaking with and make his way to Mrs. Montford. He seemed eager to talk to her, smiling broadly, but Mrs. Montford appeared reserved. She nodded her head but her smiles remained placid and infrequent. I could see she was uncomfortable, though she seemed to grow more at ease as the moments ticked by.

It made me wonder about the man at Sir Fitzwilliam's party before Christmas, who had also been eager to speak with her.

This man had a kind smile, which made his whole face light up behind his chestnut beard. He wore a smart suit of fine material and a golden chain gleamed from the front pocket of his jacket.

She certainly is quite popular with these gentlemen, is she not? I wondered. Surely, they knew that she had lost her husband. Were they merely trying to be kind and offer their condolences? Or were their intentions perhaps a bit more romantic in nature?

"I supposed I would find you ruminating," said a voice beside me.

I rounded on a familiar figure settling down into the twin of my velvet armchair.

"Mr. Jerome," I said, laying a hand over my thunderous heart. "Do not startle me so."

He chuckled, leaning back casually in his seat. "I apologize. Though I do not think I could have said anything that would not have startled you, given how lost in thought you were."

He let out a happy, long sigh beside me, irritating me further. Not only did he enjoy teasing me, he knew how flustered I had become.

"I do not imagine that you would like to spend the whole evening here in the drawing room?" he asked.

"I shall stay wherever my lady needs me," I said, shifting in my seat.

"Oh, she seems perfectly content right now," he said. "Besides, if she truly wants anything, she only need ask one of my mother's servants, of course."

I looked sidelong at him. "She expects it of me."

"Does she?" he asked, leaning forward, a glint in his blue eyes. "Or do you expect perfection of yourself?"

I felt a small twinge of anger. Was there anything wrong with being good at my job? Why did it seem as if he implied it was bad?

"I only ask because I think there is something here within my childhood home that I believe you will find very interesting," he said.

My annoyance dissipated for a brief moment when a gentle breath of curiosity pushed it away like a burst of smoke. "Such as?" I asked.

"Excellent, I knew you would come around," he said, clapping his hands together. "I would like to show you the family library."

I blinked at him. That was not at all what I had expected him to say. "The library?" I asked.

"Indeed. What say you?"

"I must remain with my mistress," I said. "She would be none too pleased if I disappeared."

"Then why don't we ask her?" he asked, getting to his feet.

I rose to follow after him. "Mr. Jerome," I said. "We should not bother her with such inane questions, especially when she is with—"

"Oh, come now," he said, walking dangerously close to the edge of the group of his mother's friends. "She will not be at all upset at us for asking her. Especially me."

My face turned scarlet, my ears and forehead burning, and I hovered near the velvet chairs, watching him draw nearer and nearer to Mrs. Montford.

I decided to follow after him, so as to be able to hear precisely what he would say to Mrs. Montford. The last thing I needed was for him to tell her something that she would question me about later, especially if it were something that I had nothing to do with.

"Good evening, Aunt Bea," Mr. Jerome said with a small bow to his aunt.

She turned, having just joined a conversation with Mrs. Townson. The two women regarded him with interest.

"Jerome," Mrs. Montford said, her expression warming. "I did not see you. Have you been here all along?"

"Yes," he said. "I was simply helping take care of something for Mother. I did have a question to ask you, though."

"I gathered," Mrs. Montford said, her eyes shifting to me as if she knew already what it was that he was going to be asking. "What is it that you need?"

"I had hoped you might give permission for your companion to accompany me to the library?" he asked.

I felt the color creep down my neck, covering my ears which burned hot. Why did he insist on making me seem so terribly foolish?

Mrs. Montford said nothing for a few moments, simply looking back and forth between the two of us. I had hoped that she would be able to see the reluctance on my face.

She is going to say no, I realized, seeing the arch in her brow. *I would not expect anything else. She will scold her nephew for asking in the first place and then scold me for—*

"Certainly," she said with a small nod, turning back to Mrs. Townson, who appeared to be as surprised as I suddenly found myself.

I felt my mouth fall open slightly. *That was not at all what I expected.*

"Very good," Mr. Jerome said with a smile. He turned to look at me. "Shall we?"

I stared at him. "I suppose so..." I said.

He held out his arm to me, leaving an intentional gap in his elbow.

I looked from his arm to his face, which looked down at me rather expectantly.

I did not want to linger there in the room, where every moment that passed would allow the eyes of the rest of the guests to drift toward us.

I slipped my hand into his arm, and at once he started toward the door, pulling me along after him.

He whisked me down the hall, a grin plastered on his handsome face. "Look here," he said, drawing up beside a portrait along the wall in the front hall. "This is my father, the late Benjamin Townson. Mother insists on keeping this hung here as a reminder to all who enter that she is not to be trifled with, lest they invoke his wrath."

"From beyond the grave?" I asked.

"Certainly not," said Mr. Jerome. "But there are allies he had that would ensure my mother's safety, me included."

"I see," I said.

"That is not all," he said. "Look here."

He gestured to the corner of the painting, where a gathering of six or so horses stood on top of a paddocked hill with a single rider among them.

"That is the Colonel," he said.

"Mrs. Montford's late husband?" I asked, moving to take a closer look.

He let out a laugh. "Indeed it is. A bit of a joke on my part, of course. Neither my mother nor father knew about it at the time."

"How ever did you accomplish it without them noticing?" I asked.

"I asked the painter to add the detail in the background and my mother seemed to like the idea well enough. She seemed to think nothing of a man who loved horses as dearly as my uncle did..." His voice trailed off. "I loved my uncle, you see, and my aunt. That is why I could not allow my mother to continue that frivolous, ceaseless feud that used to exist between her and my aunt. They have both lost too much as it is and I was not going to let them continue to waste their lives in some forgotten squabble about something that may or may not have happened."

I looked up at the distant silhouette seated upon the horse, as if guiding them all back toward the barns for the night.

"Anyway, not only do I see the proud, strong man my father was, painted in his prime, but I also have the joy of knowing that my uncle was honored in a small way as well, even if I am the only one to know it." He turned his eyes down toward me. "Well...now, I suppose it is the two of us, isn't it?"

"I suppose it is," I said. "Thank you for sharing this with me. Perhaps you should consider showing your aunt. I believe she would be quite touched with this memorialization of him."

He shook his head. "Then I would have to tell my mother. And where is the fun in that?"

He gestured toward the stairwell, which wound its way up to a second floor landing above.

"Come along, let us reach our destination before my mother sends one of the servants to call us back for dinner," he said.

He led me up the carpeted stairs, held in place by long rods of iron pressed up against the backs of the steps.

We entered into a much quieter part of the house, without another living being in sight.

"This way," he said, taking a gentle turn to the right, taking me down the hall lined with umber wallpaper and long, narrow tables filled with—

"Orchids..." I said with a small breath, gazing at the blossoms. There had to be at least two dozen plants, all in varying shades of pink and white, and a special one situated right in the middle that was a pale purple.

"Aren't they beautiful?" he asked, slowing to allow me the chance to gaze at them more closely.

I reached out and barely grazed the tips of my fingers against the soft, pink petals.

"They're lovely," I said.

He smiled. "My mother loves orchids but she has a beast of time taking care of them. I have done what I could to help propagate these and she loved the colors I bred so much that she—"

"You bred these?" I asked.

He blinked at me. "Why, yes I did," he said. "I realize it is not the sort of hobby that most men would endeavor but my mother so dearly loves them that even at a young age I tried my hand at keeping them alive for her. I learned how to care for them, and then as they grew, I had to replant them. I had little understanding as a child of how it all worked but as I found literature about them, through trial and error, I—"

He stopped and reached up to rub the back of his head, running his hand over the thick, auburn locks of his hair.

"I'm sorry," he said with a smile that, for the first time, seemed reserved. "I suppose I should not waste your time with such ridiculous—"

"It is not ridiculous," I said, looking up at him, impressed. "I know how much care and patience is involved with caring for plants." I looked at the delicate blossoms and how few existed on the waxy stems. "Your aunt has a love for them as well, you know. She only has one, which she kept in her room on her bureau. She brought it with her to London."

I looked up at him and his expression had changed to one of interest. It seemed he did not know that fact.

"Flowers may be lovely but they're also fragile," I said. "That means their care takes a great deal of patience and gentleness, both of which are valuable characteristics for anyone to learn."

He studied me, the edge of his lips curled up ever so slightly. "Thank you," he said. "I thought you might have found it rather silly."

"Not at all," I said. "I quite admire the result of all your hard work. Just look how stunning they are...how bright and healthy."

"Your appreciation means a great deal to me," he said, suddenly formal. "Well, shall we continue on?"

He gestured to the opposite side of the hall.

I allowed him to lead me across there and we stepped in through a door to a room much larger than I had expected.

Not only was it larger but it was such a strange shape, as well. Hexagonal, with a shelf at each of the eight sides of the room, along with a secondary row stacked above them reaching toward the ceiling overhead. A large mahogany desk sat in the middle of the room and two small reading nooks were arranged in separate corners. A wooden inlay filled the space in the center of the room, depicting an image of an enormous tree with a flock of birds taking flight from the branches.

"The tree of life," I said, studying it.

He nodded. "You have a keen eye," he said. "And what do you think of the statue here?"

I looked to see where he pointed and found a brilliant bronze statue, much like its twin downstairs.

"A lion," I said, walking over and laying my hand against it. "Like the one in the drawing room."

He nodded. "There are three others in the house," he said. "All are in different positions, of course."

"How interesting," I said.

"My father had them made," he said. "He admired the animals for their strength."

"Yes, they are powerful creatures," I said, my eyes lingering around the rest of the room.

"Go on then," he said, seeing my interest. "I brought you here for a reason, didn't I?"

I took a hesitant step and began to look over the spines of the books nestled away on the shelves.

"What do you think?" he asked after a few moments of silence had passed.

"It's quite a collection," I said, for once forgetting the interesting circumstances in which we found ourselves. "You and your family have an impressive variety."

"Thank you," he said. "I thought you might like it."

"I certainly do," I said.

"I had a suspicion that you are quite the reader," he said. "As often as I have caught you reading when I've come to visit."

"It is a pleasant way to spend an afternoon," I said. "Mrs. Montford prefers her days to be calm and peaceful. What better way can I give her the space that she needs?"

"Oh, I do not doubt it," he said. "You know, if there is anything here that you wish to read, please feel free to take it with you. I am certain we will see one another again soon enough and you could always return it to me then."

I said, "Oh, I could not possibly. You are very kind but I—"

"Do not fret," he said with a chuckle. "Most of these books are mine. You do not need to fear my mother."

Even so, to borrow someone else's book... I had never borrowed one of Mrs. Montford's. How could I possibly take one of his?

A sound at the door caused me to straighten at once and wheel around.

A distinguished looking older gentleman came strolling in, looking around for a moment before his eyes fell upon Mr. Jerome. "Ah, ha! There you are, lad. I have been looking for you."

I had noticed him standing among the rest of the guests downstairs, as his stature alone would have been difficult to miss. He was rather handsome, with a sharp jawline and high cheekbones. His moustache, thick and dark but lightly streaked with grey, was nearly as well-groomed as his closely trimmed hair that reminded me a great deal of the Colonel's. He strode across to Mr. Jerome, his arm extended, and the two shook hands.

"Good evening," Mr. Jerome said with a chuckle. "I apologize, sir, for not coming to greet you earlier. I simply wished to show my friend my family's library, as this is her first time here in our home."

The man turned to regard me, his thick eyebrows furrowing but a smile growing up his face. Then, he barked a laugh, a rambunctious sound that startled me. "I wondered where you two were off to, all alone," he said.

Mr. Jerome said, "Might I introduce my friend to you? This is Miss Anna Fairweather. She is here with my aunt, as her companion."

I looked over at him. While it was *technically* true, he knew as well as I that introducing me thusly was not only inaccurate, it might be considered an outright lie if someone were to take offense in the matter. And to call me his friend so easily? Considering the differences in our stations, it was certainly an unusual description.

Not for the first time, I wondered what thoughts were truly going through his mind.

Mr. Jerome did not seem flustered, though, as he looked over at me. "And may I introduce my father's old friend, as well as my aunt's, Major Lewis."

"How do you do?" Major Lewis asked with a wink

at me. "I do apologize for teasing you. You must under-stand that I cannot allow the lad to have too long for his feathers to settle. I would not be doing his late father any favors."

He clapped Mr. Jerome on the shoulder in a fatherly, affectionate way.

Then he looked at me with an arched brow. "And you are Mrs. Montford's companion? Well, I knew the late Colonel quite well, quite well indeed."

"They have all been friends for some years now," Mr. Jerome told me with a nod.

"Yes, we have indeed," Major Lewis said. "I am pleased that Mrs. Montford came this evening. I had hoped to see her soon enough."

"What did you come all the way upstairs for?" Mr. Jerome asked. "Certainly not simply to harass me?"

Major Lewis let out his bark of a laugh once more. "Well, of course," he said. "I hoped to get in a round of cards before dinner but your mother insisted I come to fetch you for the meal, lest she need to make an example of you. So, might I have your word that after dinner has concluded you will indulge me for a round or two?"

Mr. Jerome laughed. "Very well, Major, I would be glad to."

"Excellent," Major Lewis said. "Now, off we go before your mother comes to fetch us herself."

"And we would not want that," Mr. Jerome said.

We started toward the door and I glanced back over my shoulder.

"We can come back up here later," Mr. Jerome said to me with an easy smile.

I returned his smile. "All right," I said.

"Now, is it true that you plan to go see your cousins in Bath come the spring?" Major Lewis asked.

"Yes, I do," Mr. Jerome said. "It has been some time but I thought it might be nice to get out of the city for a while."

"Perhaps we will run into one another, for I am to see my sister, who—"

We never learned anything more about the Major's sister, for at that very moment, a terrible scream echoed up to us from somewhere down below.

5

"Are you all right?"

I looked up from my hands, knotted together in my lap. Mr. Jerome's face appeared in the doorway into the library where Mrs. Montford and I had taken refuge.

"We are quite all right," Mrs. Montford said but the stiffness in her voice made the knots in my stomach tighten. We were very much the opposite and we all knew it.

His brow wrinkled with worry, and he stepped into the room.

The scream had sent spikes of fear straight through my heart. As soon as I heard it, I had frozen in place, grabbing the banister of the stairwell to prevent myself from toppling down the rest of the way.

Major Lewis and Mr. Jerome had raced down the

stairs, Mr. Jerome taking two at a time. I watched as he ducked into the first door on his right, his shadow stretching out into the hallway behind him. He came to an abrupt halt upon entry.

My knees had buckled and I sat down upon the step behind me, my fingers still wrapped tightly around the banister.

I had known, even before the chaos that followed shortly after. There could only be one reason why he stopped short instead of rushing in to help. I had seen such a reaction before...

The Major followed after him and let out a shout of terror, which was quickly followed by the sound of a woman giving way to fitful wails.

I never learned who it was that had discovered the dead body, nor who had been the one to scream in the first place. All I did know was that Mrs. Montford was not in there, nor had she seen the body that had been discovered, as she had followed the group that had fled from the drawing room and down the hall toward the scream after we had all heard it.

She did not dare go into the room either, instead choosing to linger back in the hall with a few others.

The myriad voices that trickled through the doorway stumbled over one another, some in sharp terror, others in quieter murmurs of horror. The same word kept punctuating the tense moment, inflating it further.

Dead.

I went to fetch Mrs. Montford, drawing her up the stairs with me, away from the scene.

"You did not see anything, did you?" I had asked her.

Her arm trembled beneath my fingers but she shook her head, probably fighting an urge to look back over her shoulder.

Once I had squared her safely away in the library, away from the noise and mess, I chanced a look over the top of the stairs once more.

Mr. Jerome was doing his best to quell the frightened guests, urging them to stay out of his and the Major's way as they did their best to assess the situation. Mr. Jerome sent one of the servants to telephone the police, and then as if sensing my gaze, looked up the staircase and met my stare.

My jaw clenched and I could not find my voice to call down the question.

He seemed to understand, however, as he shook his head slowly, his lips pursed in distress.

The person in question—whom Mr. Jerome had identified for us as Mr. Edward Finch—had been discovered when a guest passed by on her way to the ladies room before dinner. According to Mr. Jerome, she had caught sight of a limp leg sprawled across the floor. She had gone to check on the collapsed man and the scene had petrified her so terribly that she shrieked.

That had been nearly half an hour before, every minute of which had passed by in agonizing worry as we awaited the authorities and their help in the matter.

While Mrs. Montford had said very little, she did inform me that she had been speaking with the dead man just a short time beforehand. I realized it must have been the man with the golden pocket watch and beard I had seen come to her before Mr. Jerome took me to the library.

"Are you sure you are all right?" Mr. Jerome asked, coming in to kneel beside her now. "I certainly would not at all blame you if you were a bit—"

"A bit what?" she asked. "Unsettled? Upset?"

"That and more," he said.

She sighed, shaking her head. "This never should have happened," she said. "How could it have happened?"

"No one seems to know," Mr. Jerome said with a frown. "Each person is as frightened as the next. It makes so little sense, given how close knit this group of friends is."

That much had been true. This had not been a party for just anyone. It seemed Mrs. Townson had gathered a group of her closest friends, and everyone had been getting on so well with one another just some time before.

A nagging thought pressed against my mind, though.

What is that old saying...keep your friends close but enemies closer? I wondered. Those closest to us also knew the most about us. Were not these sorts of attacks often committed by those closest to the victim?

It would make sense that it could have been someone at this party then. But who?

"Exactly what happened?" I asked.

Mr. Jerome and Mrs. Montford looked over at me. I had originally been too frightened to ask, to know, but I knew that it would come out one way or the other. I wanted it to be on my own terms and come from Mr. Jerome instead of some of the other guests.

He looked at his aunt, seemingly uncertain whether he should continue.

"He...seems to have been bludgeoned to death," he said, pressing his lips together. The color had not yet returned to his face and his comment further cemented this truth. He glanced apprehensively over his shoulder. "With one of the lion statues."

My stomach dropped as I followed his gaze to the one he and I had been commenting on earlier.

He will never look at these statues with affection ever again...

He steeled himself, however, and tried to smile at his aunt, though the expression faltered before it ever truly formed. "Apart from that, we know nothing," he said, with a bit more life in his words. I could see he was trying hard to be optimistic, for his aunt's sake and mine. "I cannot for the life of me figure out who could have wished him harm."

Heavy footsteps at the door drew my eye. I looked up to see the Major step into the room, his eyes sweeping through as they had earlier.

"Oh, Major..." Mrs. Montford said, with a voice filled with more emotion than I had seen her share since her husband's passing.

His expression softened and he hurried over to her.

She stretched her arms out to him and he took the seat beside her at once on the sofa and took her hands in his own.

"Beatrice..." he said, shaking his head. "Are you all right?" His tone, tender and gentle, caught me by surprise. It seemed contrary to a man so strong, yet I was reminded at once of Mr. Jerome's surprising care for the orchids just out in the hall. A juxtaposition, to be certain, but a welcome one, nevertheless.

She sniffed, shaking her head. "I hardly know," she said.

Without looking away, Major Lewis reached into the front pocket of his coat and withdrew a handkerchief, which he held out to her.

She took it with a tight, sad smile and dabbed at the corners of her eyes.

"I am sorry that you must endure this shock on

your own," Major Lewis said. "Without the Colonel, I mean."

Mrs. Montford folded and unfolded the handkerchief, staring at the red, embroidered *L* in the silk. "I just... I simply cannot bear the thought...of one of my husband's dearest friends being...being—"

"It's all right, dear aunt," Mr. Jerome said, reaching out to lay a hand on her shoulder. "It's all right. You do not have to say it aloud."

I bit down on the inside of my cheek until the metallic tang of blood coated my tongue.

Why had this happened again? Why must death forever occur around me?

"My husband would have been...been heartbroken," she said. "Positively so."

"As we all are," Major Lewis said in a low, gentle tone. He lifted his eyes, shaking his head. "I have seen death. I have stared it in the face but it matters not how many times you must witness it. It never becomes any easier, I am sorry to say, especially with the loss of an old friend."

"I'm sorry, Aunt, I did not realize that you and Mr. Finch were as close as you were," Mr. Jerome said.

"Oh, we all were," Mrs. Montford said with an angry sniff, waving the handkerchief in front of her face. "All of us, for many years."

"Almost forty now, isn't it?" Major Lewis asked. "Good heavens, has it really been that long?"

Mrs. Montford looked up at him, and just as I had the night her husband had passed, I saw a much younger, much more frightened woman sitting before me. "Since you both served together, yes," she said.

"I am sorry that I never made it out to Maidstone," Major Lewis said, shaking his head. "All those years, I should have—"

"No, Major, you do not need to apologize," Mrs. Montford said, shaking her head, laying her hand on his arm. "Please, we have enough now to deal with, what with Mr. Finch..."

"Beatrice, what sort of friend have I been?" Major Lewis asked. "When something this horrific could have happened at any moment? All the time I have wasted."

It startled me to hear him call her by her first name. Until today, I had never heard of this man. Until today, he was a stranger to me.

It reminded me how much of Mrs. Montford's life I truly was not privy to.

A few tears splashed down her cheek and she did nothing to stem them. "Then we must do our best to make the most of our time from now on," she said. "We owe it to them all."

Major Lewis then turned his gaze to Mr. Jerome. "We certainly do owe it to our loved ones," he said, his expression hardening. "And we owe it to Mr. Finch to find who is responsible for this heinous act so we'll know who to point out to the police, when they arrive."

"I could not agree more," Mr. Jerome said, his own face hardening. "But at this moment, I imagine your guess would be as good as mine."

"Of which I have none," Major Lewis said, his brow furrowed as he swiped his fingers over his thick moustache. "I have a difficult time imagining it could have been anyone here. How could any of his friends have done him in like this?"

"I do not know," Mrs. Montford said, disappearing behind the handkerchief once more, a stifled sob the only other sound I could hear.

"Who would have been in the study?" Major Lewis asked. "Perhaps any of the staff?"

"I do not know," Mr. Jerome said, "as Anna and I were up here, with you, when the deed must have been committed."

Major Lewis frowned, looking down.

He rose to his feet and began to walk with long strides across the room. "Do you know if your mother has hired anyone new to work around the house or garden? Or perhaps the housekeeper would know?"

"It seems unlikely. I believe Mother would have discussed changes to the staff with me," Mr. Jerome said, also getting to his feet, his expression worried.

Major Lewis stopped and regarded him. "I apologize for perhaps coming across as uncaring but I spent years training for difficult situations. Shock wears off quickly and it is best to focus on the task at hand, which in this case is finding the murderer."

"Of course," Mr. Jerome said, seemingly steeling himself, his voice now harboring a bit more strength. He looked at his aunt. "Do you remember anyone leaving the drawing room?"

"It's hard to say," Mrs. Montford said. "I suppose I was not paying much attention to who might have been coming and going. Why would I have been? Just a short time ago, it was a party, not an investigation."

"True enough," Mr. Jerome said. He let out a heavy sigh. "I suppose all there is left to do is get everyone back together and see what they all might know."

"Quite right," Major Lewis said, starting toward the door. "I certainly hope someone saw something. I only wish we might have left the library a moment sooner. Perhaps we could have caught the culprit as they fled the scene."

Mr. Jerome's face fell. "Perhaps we could have."

"Mr. Jerome, are you there?" someone called up the stairs. "A police sergeant has arrived."

Mr. Jerome straightened. "Pardon me, if you will," he said to all of us. With a graceful pivot, he disappeared out of the room.

"I should go with him," Major Lewis said, taking long strides to the door. "I want to see what I can do to offer any help."

I watched him follow after Mr. Jerome, my heart heavy.

They left the room in a thick silence that seemed to press in against me with a ringing in my ears.

I glanced over at Mrs. Montford, who had said very little apart from speaking to Major Lewis.

"I'm sorry, Mrs. Montford," I said. "I had no idea that this man was so close to you."

Mrs. Montford's lip trembled and she nodded. "It's all right," she said, gathering herself. "Though I must admit, I am beginning to worry that this trail of tragedy wherever we go will somehow never end."

My throat grew tight and I shook my head at once. "No, Mrs. Montford, you should not worry like that," I said. "It is superstitious thinking. One death does not beget another."

"One would think not," Mrs. Montford said, staring down at the floor.

I found that I did not have the strength, nor the heart, to say anything more.

6

It was well after midnight by the time we were allowed to make our way home. The police sergeant, a rather unhelpful man, did nothing more than bark questions at everyone in the house. The men he brought along with him examined the body in the study down the hall, ultimately removing it from the home.

When no one came forth with any information, the police suggested a possibility that the killer had been an intruder who had somehow sneaked in and out of the place without being seen, except by the dead man who might have been killed for walking in on an attempted theft. While no one else seemed to have any better idea or explanation, it did nothing to help ease anyone's nerves. We were left with no answers and with only Mr. Finch's body as evidence that anything had occurred at all, at least until the police finished their investigation, whenever that might be.

After the police had gone, Major Lewis and some of the other men who had been guests that evening offered to stay and protect the home, lest the culprit try to return and do further harm. Mr. Jerome seemed relieved at their offer, and it gave me peace to know that he and his mother would not be alone.

Poor Mrs. Townson had been utterly stunned to silence about the whole matter. All I had heard her say the whole night were three words: "In...my home?"

Mr. Jerome seemed to be holding himself together well enough but his usual cheer had disappeared entirely, replaced with a steely resolve that was only matched by that of Major Lewis.

Mrs. Montford and I returned home, where I managed to fall asleep around three in the morning and awoke before five.

I rose and dressed and began my daily tasks long before I met any others on the staff, lost in my own thoughts. My mind kept returning to the events of the night before.

How many minutes had passed since Mr. Jerome and I had walked by that study on our way to the library? We could not have been gone from the drawing room for more than a quarter of an hour, at most. How could anything so horrific have happened in such a short space of time? How had no one noticed?

The pain-stricken faces of Mrs. Montford, Major Lewis, and Mrs. Townson played over and over again in my mind. I had never met this Mr. Finch, but the anguish that I could see in each of them suggested a close friendship had indeed existed between them all.

Mrs. Montford seemed most distressed of all. To lose a close friend so soon after losing her husband... I kept seeing the horror in her eyes. She had not yet begun to grieve the loss of Mr. Finch before she had surely begun to worry that she would lose someone else. Who passed through her mind? Mrs. Baird, her friend from Brighton? Lady Fitzwilliam? Perhaps Mrs. Townson?

Mr. Jerome?

I pushed those thoughts aside, realizing it did me no good to dwell on them. They were morbid, of course, and it was not as if thinking about them would bring them into existence. That made no sense and was not at all logical.

I made my way to Mrs. Montford's room just before seven, doing my best to keep myself in good spirits, if only for her peace of mind. I did not know whether to even address what had happened the night before. I felt it would be best if I tried to maintain as normal a behavior as possible for her...and for myself.

I strode into the room, making my way over to the
drapes after closing the door gently behind myself.

*Nothing has changed. Everything is just the same as it
always is. We are simply going to go about our day as if
nothing is different. Not anything at all.*

I reached up to grab hold of the thick velvet drapes
covering the windows and slowly drew them open.

A foggy, grey scene greeted me, with bleak, pale
light and frost clinging to the corners of the window
panes.

My heart sank. We could certainly have done with
some sunshine.

"Good morning, Mrs. Montford," I said, trying my
best to keep up a positive attitude, even when I felt
nothing at all like it. "It is just after seven."

The rustle of blankets told me she heard me but
she said nothing.

I gave her some space, moving to her wardrobe and
drawing the doors open. I looked through the right
side of the rack, looking for something she had not
worn terribly recently. I selected a blue dress as well as
a charcoal grey one with long sleeves. I avoided black. I
knew that might be far too stark of a reminder for her
for the time being.

Normal. Help it remain normal.

"I believe Mr. Fitzroy has received the tea that your
cousin spoke of in her letter to you at Christmas," I
said, laying the dresses side by side over the fainting

couch at the foot of her bed. "And I believe that you are scheduled to see Lady Fitzwilliam at noon. She is coming for luncheon."

"I do not wish to have any visitors today," Mrs. Montford said, sitting up slowly.

With a skip of my heart, I realized that she was struggling to rise.

"Mrs. Montford, are you all right?" I asked, hurrying over.

She threw out her arm to stop me and looked up at me with a glare.

The skin beneath her eyes had puffed and swollen and her eyes were tinged with red.

"I am perfectly all right, girl," she snapped, as she righted herself, swinging her legs over the side of the mattress.

I studied her. "Are you certain?" I asked.

"I am as well as I am able to be right now," she said, glaring at me. "Now, fetch my robe."

I turned to take her robe off the hook along the wall and helped her shrug it up onto her shoulders.

Without another word, she walked to the front of the bed and looked down at the choices I had laid out for her.

I stayed back near the edge of the bed where I began to make up the quilts and pillows.

Had I somehow spoken out of turn? Had the last few weeks of shared troubles caused me to become too comfortable around her, letting my guard down, believing that I had more familiarity with her than I truly did?

No, that was not it.

Mrs. Montford was hurting and I was taking her reaction far too personally.

She stood staring down at the dresses and it was not long before I realized that the vacant stare she wore had nothing at all to do with choosing the attire she was to wear for the day.

I wanted to ask what she was thinking, what troubled her most, but I knew how futile it would be. I knew it was not my place.

It must have been terrible for her to wake up with the realization that she had not yet come to grips with her husband's death before she had to endure the death of a friend, as well.

Mrs. Montford said nothing else to me as I helped her get ready for the day. I pinned her hair back in a simple silver pin with an inlay of pearls. I brushed her hair as diligently as I ever did but she did not meet my gaze in the reflection of the mirror of her vanity.

I felt as if we were strangers by the time we went down for her breakfast.

I draped her napkin over her lap as George came teetering into the dining room with a tray stacked high with plates. "Here we are," he said, gently lowering the tray to the edge of the table. He lifted the top plate and set before Mrs. Montford a handsome slice of ham with thick gravy and a side of baked beans. "Something to warm you this morning, ma'am."

Mrs. Montford gave him an indignant sniff but she did not send the food, or him, away.

I breathed a small sigh of relief before I made my way to a chair in the corner near the fireplace. George gave me a worried look as he passed by me through the door into the kitchen.

The fog pressed in against the windows, obscuring the trees even a short distance away, their empty branches like fingers scraping against the thick air that seemed as dense as a cloud. I watched it for a moment, the eerie stillness, the indistinguishable passing of time, as there was no sun and hardly any light to speak of. It was not at all the sort of day for travel or shopping. I hoped that Mrs. Montford would choose to remain indoors, though given her attitude, I could not imagine her wanting anything else.

A tap at the door was greeted with Mrs. Montford's steely request for entry.

Mr. Fitzroy stepped inside with a bow. "Good morning, ma'am. Your nephew is here to see you."

Mrs. Montford glared at him, partway through a bite of her breakfast. "This early?" she asked, pressing a napkin to her lips. She made an indistinct sound like a grunt and nodded. "Very well," she said. "Let him in."

Mr. Jerome's face appeared around Mr. Fitzroy as

soon as she gave the word. "Good morning, Aunt Bea. I am glad that you are allowing me to see you."

Mrs. Montford's expression hardened, as she smoothed her napkin back across her lap.

"What do you want?" she asked. "I have little patience for trivial matters. Unless you come with the news that I am looking for, you are wasting your time."

Mr. Jerome gave his aunt a patient, sad look as he remained near to the door. His eyes shifted back to me and I could see the worry in his gaze.

"Well, if you are hoping that I come with the news of who killed Mr. Finch, then...I have not," he said cautiously.

Mrs. Montford glared at him and simply remained silent.

He took a few steps toward her, his expression softening. "My dear aunt, I am terribly sorry about what has happened. To lose a friend in such a—"

"Do not pity me," she said, her voice growing louder. It echoed briefly against the crystal of the chandelier overhead and the glass of the windows. "You do not begin to know my pain," she went on. "What I have had to endure these past many weeks."

"No, I certainly do not," Mr. Jerome said. "But there is someone who, unfortunately, does know. And she sits in this room."

An uncomfortable stillness settled over the room.

I sat as stiff as a cornered bird on a branch, staring up at Mr. Jerome. Why on *earth* had he—

Mrs. Montford slowly turned her chair, her eyes shifting to me.

I expected to see the same heated frustration that I had seen earlier this morning, the same anger.

Yet I saw only...sorrow? Pity?

"Anna has carried these burdens as well, sometimes having to witness death itself. She, more than anyone, has seen and felt what you have," Mr. Jerome went on. "I hope that you will both give one another some comfort at such a time."

Mrs. Montford stared at me as if seeing me for the first time.

I did not know what to say and so I said nothing, instead looking away, my face burning hot.

"Well..." Mrs. Montford said after a long, heavy stretch of silence. "Why are you here this morning, then?"

"I did come with some news," Mr. Jerome said, taking the seat beside her at the table. "And I did hope that Anna would come and listen as well, as this concerns her."

My chin rose and my eyes narrowed. Me?

Mrs. Montford sighed. "Very well. Girl, come over here."

I rose and walked to the tableside, where I looked as calmly as I could over at Mr. Jerome. "Yes?"

"I am in need of some assistance," he said. "I realize Mr. Finch was a dear friend of yours, Aunt Bea."

Mrs. Montford straightened, sniffing. "Go on then, what do you need?"

"The servant last night who burst into tears at the sight of Mr. Finch's body?" he asked. "Well, I had hoped that—"

"One moment, Jerome," Mrs. Montford said, raising a hand in question. "What servant? We heard nothing of this."

He hesitated, looking from her back to me. "You did not?" he asked. "One of the housemaids, Ginny, came through the back door into the study last night, entirely unaware of the happenings, and stumbled upon Mr. Finch. This was before the police had removed the body." He shook his head. "She seemingly lost her mind at the sight, falling to the floor and weeping hysterically. It would be a distressing sight for anyone who was unprepared, of course, but her reaction seemed extreme for a young woman who didn't have any connection to the deceased."

"And...?" Mrs. Montford prompted. "Are you suggesting she might know something?"

"That is what I would like to find out," he said, folding his hands in front of him. He looked back and forth between the two of us. "It seems possible there was some sort of connection between the two of them, a connection that both my mother and I were unaware of."

"What sort of connection?" Mrs. Montford asked, her brow furrowing into a single, angry line.

"That is what I am hoping to discover," he said.

"Was Mr. Finch a frequent guest at your home?" I asked.

"Yes," Mr. Jerome said, with a nod. "He certainly was. Since my father died, he often stopped by to have dinner with us, saying my father would have wished him to keep an eye on us and our needs."

"And you believe he might have met your house-maid during those visits?" Mrs. Montford asked.

Mr. Jerome said, "Maybe. It is entirely possible that she knew something of him that he did not want known, or perhaps he caught her doing something she wishes to hide. We don't know."

"Why don't you ask her, then?" Mrs. Montford asked, her sharp, cutting tone returning. "Why waste time coming all the way down here to muse about possibilities and theories?"

"That is not the only reason why I have come," he said. He looked over at me. "I had hoped to see if Anna could accompany me back to the house to speak to the young woman herself."

Mrs. Montford seemed as surprised as I was.

"Me?" I asked.

"Why do you need her?" Mrs. Montford asked.

"The maid is close to Anna's age and both are servants in wealthy households. Perhaps she will feel comfortable enough to speak with Anna, while finding others too intimidating."

"She is not speaking to you?" I asked.

"I'm afraid not," he said. "I tried last night but she shut herself in her room. Short of breaking the door down, there was little I could do."

"*Did* you break the door down?" Mrs. Montford asked.

"Certainly not," Mr. Jerome said, giving her a surprised look.

"You are looking for a murderer, boy," she said. "How can you expect to find anything out if you aren't willing to—"

"I realized there was a far more peaceable option," he said. "One that would not terrify the poor girl but would get me the information I want."

"And what of the police?" she asked. "Did they not question her, as well?"

"Oh, they certainly tried," he said. "She was unable to pull herself together, in hysterics. Eventually, they became so frustrated at her incessant crying that they sent her away to speak with the next member of our staff. The girl's been locked up in her room ever since. No one but me thinks her of significance."

Mrs. Montford huffed. "What makes you think she will speak to Anna at all?"

"It is only a hunch," he said. "But I have no other ideas."

Dread filled me. The last thing I wanted was to be drawn into the investigation of another murder. Not after the last time. Or the time before...

"What say you, Anna?"

My eyes snapped up to his. "Your housemaid does not know me," I pointed out. "There is no reason to believe she would consider speaking with me in the first place."

"Too true," Mrs. Montford said with a nod. "Best to send for the police again."

"You saw what good that did us last night," Mr. Jerome said. "That utter fool of a police sergeant believes whoever killed Mr. Finch was some stranger, a burglar perhaps, who fled the house while no one was looking."

Mrs. Montford's eyes narrowed. "And you do not agree? Do you suppose it was someone at the party last night?"

"Who else could it have been?" he asked. "This servant is our only lead at the moment, the only one who has behaved suspiciously. She is the best place—and the only place—that we can start. Perhaps she can point us in a different direction but we will not know unless we get some information out of her."

Mrs. Montford shifted uneasily in her chair. "Perhaps it is best to leave this alone, Jerome," she said in a low voice. She adjusted the shawl she wore, bringing it closer to her neck as if to cover herself more fully. "Mr. Finch...he..."

"I know," Mr. Jerome said. "Mother tried to tell me the same. It is entirely possible that in his line of work, he might have made enemies."

"Line of work?" I asked aloud. "What did he do?"

"He was a businessman and a craftsman of sorts," Mr. Jerome said. "Specialized in leatherwork. He made quite a number of the pieces in my mother's home, including the chairs in the library. His passion, however, was helping to outfit the military. He made and sold slings for rifles."

"That is interesting," I said. "Such an odd piece to focus on."

"Not really," he said. "He would make them only for the officers, as they often had specific requests for theirs."

"That doesn't seem particularly dangerous," I said.

"You wouldn't think so but he was a shrewd, stubborn man who could drive a hard bargain. Not everybody liked that about him. His friends respected him, however. He was a master of his trade." Mr. Jerome shook his head. "He was knowledgeable and talented. It's certainly a shame that he is gone now."

He looked up at his aunt. "I am sorry, Aunt. I did not mean to—"

"Enough," Mrs. Montford said, getting to her feet,

the legs of her chair screeching against the wooden floor as it slid back. "You may take Anna with you. But she is not to be gone for long. She has duties to attend to here."

Mr. Jerome's head swiveled as he looked up at the clock. "Very well. I shall have her home within a few hours."

"See that you do."

She glared at him and then at me, before she started off toward the door, the *click, clack, click* of her heeled shoes following after her as she left.

"I have never seen her like this," Mr. Jerome said in a low voice.

"Nor I," I said. "At least, not quite so severe. Not with you, anyway."

He gave me a steady look. "Is she all right?"

I stole a quick glance out the door. "I am not entirely sure," I said. "She seemed terribly weak this morning, but when I tried to help, she became angry and would not allow me near her. She has treated me as if I have wronged her in some way."

"No, not you," he said with a shake of his auburn head. "The world has wronged her and she is beside herself, not knowing what to do about it."

"I suppose..." I said.

"Perhaps learning what that housemaid knows will give us all some peace," he said. "Are you ready to go?"

He rose to his feet.

"As ready as I can be," I said. "Precisely what is it that you would have me do?"

"I would like you to go in and ask her some questions. Tell her who you are, that you are employed by my aunt. I imagine she will trust you more than she would me or anyone else."

"You mean because I am also a servant?"

"Yes," he said. "You—being who and what you are —are a great deal less threatening than the master of the house coming around with questions about a murder."

"But what will I tell her is my reason for being there?" I asked. "Surely she will see through any ruse that I might concoct."

"I do not expect you to lie to her," he said. "All we really want is to learn what we can about her relationship with Mr. Finch. I do believe this is the best option we have."

I looked down, my heart beginning to race.

"I should tell you, there is an additional reason I want to get to the bottom of all this quickly," he said in a low voice. "My mother has been badly distressed. She swore to me last night that she would not remain in that house while there was a killer running loose."

I looked up at him. "Did she leave last night?"

He nodded. "After everyone else left, I escorted her across town to the home of Lady Fitzwilliam, who welcomed her." He sighed, shaking his head. "I'm rather afraid that she will not step foot back in our home ever again. I do not know if learning the truth will change that. Even if it doesn't, I must know what occurred beneath my family's roof and ensure the killer does not get away with such a crime."

"I suppose I can understand why you feel personally invested," I said. "Mr. Finch was a guest in your home and a friend to your family. I shall help you, if I can."

"Excellent," he said. "We have not a moment to waste."

7

The Townson house seemed strangely hollow upon our arrival. A place that had been warm and bustling and full of laughter the night before now boasted nothing more than empty, cold fireplaces and echoing, dark rooms and corridors. The house felt enormous and shallow. We might as well have been stepping inside a museum.

Mr. Jerome did not take me past the study, for which I was incredibly grateful. Instead, he steered me to the right of the dining room, toward the kitchen, where he located one of the few servants who still remained to tend the house. I supposed the others had left, much like the mistress of the house herself.

"Becky, this is Anna," Mr. Jerome said. "She is my aunt's personal maid. Please take her to speak with Maddie."

"Right away, Mr. Townson," the girl said with a small curtsy.

She turned somewhat mechanically and started down the hall.

With a short, quick glance back at Mr. Jerome, I followed after her.

When we made our way around the corner, she looked at me and dropped her voice. "Why are you here?" she asked.

"I was in the house when Mr. Finch was found dead," I said. "And I heard how terribly Maddie has been taking it. I want to help."

"She certainly has been distressed," Becky said. "You are going to try and get some sense out of her?"

"I hope so, yes," I said. "Have any of you spoken with her yet?"

Becky shook her head. "No," she said. "She has refused to speak to anyone. She is too distraught."

I frowned. "Do you think she will agree to see me, then?"

Becky shrugged. "I do not know," she said. "I suppose the best thing we could do is try. I think she needs to speak about what happened. It is clearly upsetting her."

She took me to Maddie's room and gave me a wary look as we approached the door. She knocked a few times, and we waited for an answer.

At first, we heard nothing.

"Maddie?" Becky called, rubbing her palms together, as if nervous. "Are you there?"

A whimper echoed through the door. "Y-Yes..." came the small, stuffy voice of a woman who sounded as if she had been crying for some time.

"There is someone here to see you," Becky said. "She wants to speak with you and try to help you."

"No, tell them to go away," Maddie said with a hitch in her voice. "I do not want to speak with the police."

My heart skipped, as I stepped up to the door. "Do not worry, I am not with the police," I said. "I am a friend."

A quiet stillness greeted me.

"Maddie?" I asked.

"You...are not with the police?" she asked, sounding tentative.

"No," I said. "I am a servant, just like you."

More silence.

"My name is Anna Fairweather," I said. "I am ladies maid to Mr. Jerome's aunt, Mrs. Montford."

"Mrs. Montford," she murmured. She must have recognized the name.

"Might I come in?" I asked. "I believe I am... uniquely suited to speak with you about what you witnessed last night."

All the way to Mr. Jerome's home, I had not known what I would say to this young woman to convince her to trust me. I had gone back and forth on a number of choices. It was not until I stood at her door that I knew it was truth that would win the day. I was uniquely able to understand the shock of being near an unexpected, violent death. This might be the only chance I had to learn something, and so far, it seemed that the maid was willing to speak. I did not know if it would stay that way, but for now, I was doing what I had told Mr. Jerome I would.

"All right," Maddie said, relenting. "But—but you may only stay for a few moments. No more. If I think that you are...you are lying to me, then you will be asked to leave."

"Very well," I said. "May I come in?"

"Yes," Maddie said.

I stepped into her room, which she must have shared with two others, given the long, narrow beds lined up along the wall.

I looked around and thought at first that the space must be empty. As small as the room was, with a simple bureau with a wash basin next to the door, a single writing desk, and a wardrobe near the far side, I was amazed that I did not see her immediately.

I had almost begun to think she had sneaked out the window, when I heard the creak of a floorboard and turned to see her near the window.

She was a thin young woman with pale hair that reminded me of strands of wheat, a long face, and eyes of ice blue.

"Hello," she said, hunching her shoulders, inclining her head. She was probably near my age but something in her face made her seem younger.

"Hello," I said in return.

"You said you could help me?" She reached up to adjust the black shawl that she had wrapped around her shoulders.

A shawl for mourning? I wondered. That seemed rather overdramatic, under the circumstances. But then, it seemed there might be more to the circumstances than I yet knew.

"I hope to help, yes," I said.

"Why?" she asked.

I knew it was not wise to dance around the subject. "You were quite affected by Mr. Finch's death, were you not?" That certainly was a mild way of saying that she had wept bitterly at the sight of his corpse, the way that Mr. Jerome had described it.

At once, her hand leapt to her lips, which trembled. She sniffed and nodded, seemingly trying to gather herself. "Yes," she said. "I was."

"I see." I said.

She gave me a hard look. "Do you really? Have you ever lost someone you cared for? And so violently?"

"I have," I said. "And given how distraught you have been over Mr. Finch's death, you certainly must have cared for him a great deal."

"Is that why Mr. Townson sent you to see me?" she

asked. "To learn about my...acquaintance with Mr. Finch?"

"Yes, I believe so," I said. "Would you mind telling me what it is that you are so afraid to tell anyone else?"

She stared at me like a frightened rabbit cornered in a garden.

This must have been what the police had encountered, perhaps with more weeping.

"I realize this must be very difficult for you," I said.

"You are not here on behalf of the police, are you?" she asked, her voice barely above a whisper.

"No," I said, shaking my head. "Mr. Townson realized that you might be too afraid to speak with him or his mother, given your position within their household."

"Why do they not wish to leave me in peace?" she asked, drawing her shoulders in to herself. "Can I not simply grieve without being disturbed?"

Her erratic change in mood shook me a bit. "I thought you wished to speak of it?" I asked.

She shook her head, a fresh stream of tears washing down her cheeks. "Oh, I hardly know," she said, pressing her palms flat against the sides of her face. "I am...so ashamed."

Ashamed? Why was she feeling ashamed?

She sank down into the chair beside the window and buried her face in her hands, a wave of sobs emanating from her frail frame.

I fought the urge to flee the room, feeling both sympathetic and also somewhat annoyed that she was so terribly overcome.

What to do? What am I to do?

She relented for a moment, withdrawing her hands to fetch a handkerchief from the windowsill, which she promptly blew her nose into.

"I am terribly sorry," she said. "I-I have not been myself since...since he—"

I took slow steps toward her, trying to empathize with her suffering.

"It's all right," I said. "I only wish that I could have brought some comforting, encouraging news."

"How could you?" she asked, folding and unfolding the handkerchief in her hands. "Apart from bringing news that perhaps Mr. Finch was not truly..." She could not bring herself to say the word.

"I wish I could," I said. "But that is part of the reason I have come. To help find out who is responsible for what happened to him."

She turned an angry look on me. "I thought you said you were not working with the police?"

"I am not," I said. "I promise you. I am not."

Her furrowed brow did not smooth.

"I am hoping to find the answers for Mrs. Townson and Mr. Jerome," I said. "So that this house can have some sort of peace for all of you. Mr. Finch was a dear friend of Mrs. Townson, as well as my mistress, Mrs. Montford. His death has rattled us all."

She gave me a wary look, wrinkling the handkerchief between her fingers. "I suppose I had not thought of how it would affect my mistress..."

"Sometimes it is difficult to see outside of oneself when grieving so deeply," I suggested.

She sniffed. "What do you want to know?" she asked.

"What do you want to tell me?"

"Where would I begin?" She sounded exasperated.

"Were you and Mr. Finch...involved in a romantic relationship?" I guessed.

It seemed an unlikely idea, considering there was clearly a gap of several decades between their ages, but such things did not bother some women. Besides, it would explain her grief.

She looked up at a distant spot on the far wall. Her expression became blank.

"I suppose one might call it a secret romance," she said, her voice devoid of emotion. "He proposed marriage to me, three weeks ago. He said that, come February, he would have tied up all his loose ends and completed a contract that would settle some debts, so that we might start fresh and be married. He was not a terribly wealthy man, like some in his social circle, you see."

Yet comfortably enough off to attract the attention of an

ambitious young housemaid who didn't want to be a servant forever?

I wondered if the suspicion was unkind or simply accurate. I did not know this girl well enough to be sure.

"I take it that Mrs. Townson was unaware of your relationship?" I asked.

"Yes, well, I suppose he would not have told her, would he?" she asked. "He would have been frightened that it would make its way back to his wife, whom he had long been planning to divorce for her own infidelity."

"He was married?" I asked, wondering how word of that had escaped me.

She nodded. "Yes, that was one of the *loose ends* I spoke of. He was going to tell her he was leaving her."

"When?" I asked.

"Soon," she said. "He promised me this time he would tell her and that would be the end of it. He had made that promise before but I believe he did mean it this time."

"Did his wife ever know about you?" I asked.

I wondered if, in the betrayed wife, I had already found a possible suspect with obvious motive.

But Maddie shook her head. "No," she said, her eyes widening. "She was never to know about me until much, much later. He said that we would do everything the right way. He was determined to marry me.

He kissed me only once in all the time I knew him. His wife...I only ever saw her on a few occasions, when I somehow found them both sitting here in Mrs. Townson's parlor. A rare occurrence, as she usually despised going anywhere with him. She struck me as a most wretched character. It was known by many people that she preferred the company of other men over that of her husband. Even he knew it but put up with it for years."

Her impression of the wife could very well be colored by her own situation, I realized, but I held my tongue. I still had some questions.

"How did the two of you meet?"

"At Mrs. Townson's birthday party three and a half years ago," she said. "I spilled a drink on him and he followed me down to the kitchen where I tried to remove the stain from his tie. That was how we first became acquainted and things slowly developed from there."

She rose and stared out the window. The dim light filtering in made her look as if she were made of stone. The stains from her tears gleamed like small rivulets upon her cheeks.

Either her grief was real or she was a good actress, I thought.

"I realize how terrible this all must seem," she said. "Do you not see how I have wanted to keep this information private?"

"Yet you are telling me," I said. "Why did you decide to tell me?"

"Because I am…" she said, looking down. "I am so terribly frightened."

"Frightened?" I asked. "Frightened of what?"

"Frightened the authorities will think that I killed him."

I stared at her. "Is there any reason they should think that?" I asked carefully.

"Because of our secret engagement," she said, and I could see the tremors had started to grow stronger. "It will surely be used against me."

Her fear seemed genuine.

She said, "They might think that I killed him out of jealousy, or perhaps as a means of ensuring that if I could not have him, then his wife could not, either."

I stared at her. Was that true? Would she have so openly admitted to it?

"Don't you see?" she asked, taking a hasty step toward me, nearly upending her chair. "It would be so easy for them to pin it all on me! But I did not do it! I am innocent!"

Her voice had begun to rise in volume. She grabbed hastily at the front of her dress, clawing it as if it were suffocating her.

"Easy now," I said, holding my hands aloft. "I have never accused you of such a thing."

"Yes, but they surely will," she said. "As soon as

they learn of our relationship, they...they will suspect me. I have done wrong, in the eyes of everyone, even myself. Why should they believe me when I say I am innocent?"

"I loved Mr. Finch," she continued, her voice cracking. "I would never—*never*—do anything so...so heinous. Why would I kill the man I love?"

I stared at the girl. She did not strike me as a crazed killer bent on revenge and fueled by jealousy. I could not imagine this weepy, somewhat hysterical young woman raising a statue of a lion and bludgeoning a man in the skull with it.

"What was the last conversation you had with him?" I asked.

She looked distraught and the distance in her gaze made it obvious that she was reliving the moment. "The night he died," she said. "Before heading through the front door, he sneaked around to the kitchens and sent for me. He and I spoke out in the alleyway for a few moments."

"What did he say to you?" I asked. "Was there anything strange in his conversation? Did he mention anything that might indicate he was in any danger?"

"No, not at all," she said, shaking her head. "In fact, he seemed rather pleased. He told me that he had made some decisions that had freed him from something that could have proved quite disastrous. He told me he would explain it all later but that he was beginning to feel as if everything had fallen into place for us. He simply needed to finalize the terms of his divorce with his lawyer and then we would be on our merry way."

I felt a stirring of sympathy for the girl. I did not wish to tell her that it was quite possible Mr. Finch was stringing her along. Anyway, how could I know? Perhaps he had been telling her the truth. And perhaps her affection for him had been real and not born of a simple desire to escape her low position in life.

"Did you quarrel with him?" I asked.

"No, not once," Maddie said, her expression stricken. "He was always so kind to me. I did not kill him. How could I ever? My whole life has been *ruined*. I am *ruined*."

"There, now..." I said. "All is not lost."

"Have you ever loved someone so?" she asked, the tears returning as she looked at me. "So much that your own life seems to mean nothing apart from his?"

Unbidden, a memory passed through my mind of Mr. Jerome catching my eye across a room full of people, his look holding me like the weight of an anchor. A look meant for *me* and no one else. I quickly shook the thought aside. It was a ridiculous one.

"I shall never love again," she said, hanging her head.

"For now, you surely will not," I said. "It will take time but your heart will heal."

"No," Maddie said, wrapping her arms tightly around herself. "No, I never shall."

There would be no convincing her and now was not the time for it.

"You do realize that this information needs to be shared, yes?" I asked.

Maddie did not meet my eye, nor did she say anything.

"Would you be willing to speak with the police?" I asked.

"Why?" she asked.

"To clear your name," I said. "If you agree to help them, perhaps point them in the direction of someone else who might have had some sort of poor relationship with Mr. Finch, then it is possible they could find the one responsible for his untimely death."

She pursed her lips, and I realized my error in saying it so flippantly.

"Will it mean that his wife will find out?" she asked. "How can I be certain that she will not try to kill *me*?"

"I do not know," I said. "There is a great deal that I cannot promise you or make known to you. But I believe you will ultimately be safest, and look less suspicious, if you tell the police everything you have just told me."

"To be perfectly honest, I feel somewhat relieved

already," she said. "The fear I have been carrying around... I have not been able to breathe."

"Well, I am pleased that our conversation has helped you, even just a little," I said.

She nodded and seemed to gather herself, looking over at me, eyelashes still glittering with tears. "I will speak with the authorities," she said. "I cannot cower here any longer while whoever it was that killed my love has...has gone free."

"And if his wife learns everything?" I asked.

"Then I suppose she will learn," she said. "Perhaps it is best if she finally knows the truth."

I nodded. "Very well," I said. "I must go now, Maddie, but I hope that you find the peace you need right now."

"You believe me, don't you?" she asked.

"I do believe you," I said, hiding any flicker of doubt. I knew it was best to keep such uncertainties to myself, for now.

She let out a breath. "Thank you," she said.

I started toward the door.

"Please tell Mr. Townson that I am...sorry," she said.

"You have nothing to apologize for," I said.

"I am afraid you are wrong," she said. "When I share the truth, then I will have a great deal that I must apologize for."

I left the room, closing the door behind myself. I

knew there was nothing more I could do to help the girl. She had made the decisions she had made and now she would have to live with the consequences she faced.

At the very least, she recognizes that she must make some difficult decisions and have some hard conversations in the coming days in order to salvage what she can of her reputation, I thought.

"What happened?" I looked up to see Mr. Jerome appear around the corner.

"What did she say?" he asked.

I glanced behind me at her door. "That she is innocent," I said.

"And do you believe her?" he asked.

"I would like to. She seems an unlikely culprit but it is impossible to be sure," I said.

I looked up the hall, and he seemed to understand.

"Oh, yes, let us move away," he said.

He stopped outside an open doorway, and when I peered inside, I realized we were standing just outside the larder.

"No one will overhear us in here," he said.

I stepped in and he came in after me, closing the door after him.

The darkness of the enclosed space seeped in, apart from the small square window on the back wall, partially hidden by a shelf stacked with boxes.

"Well?" he asked, turning to me. "What did you learn? Did she confide in you?"

I opened my mouth to speak and then I realized...

"I...cannot say," I said.

He blinked at me. "You what?"

"I am sorry, Mr. Jerome," I said firmly. "But her story is not mine to tell. She has agreed to speak with the authorities but, until then, I do not wish to potentially endanger her by saying more."

He surveyed me. "Endanger her?" he asked.

"Yes," I said. "If the killer is anyone but her, Maddie's secrets could put her in harm's way."

He stared at me, his brow furrowing. "You are not going to tell me what she said to you?"

"Not right now," I said. "Not before the police speak with her."

His eyes bored into mine, as if he might be able to learn the truth by discerning it from my gaze alone.

"You truly think me learning the information would put her at risk?" he asked. "Perhaps you think it is I who cannot be trusted?"

"It isn't like that," I protested. "I only mean that the more people who know, the further word may spread. If it were to reach particular people prematurely, then we might very well have an even bigger problem on our hands."

He nodded, although his expression was reluctant. "Very well," he said. "I trust your judgment. I hope you realize that. If it were anyone else, anyone at all, I would be demanding answers."

I knew he spoke the truth. "I understand," I said.

"I shall go and have a word with the authorities after I take you back to my aunt," he said. "I hope we will soon be able to resolve all of this."

"I do as well," I said.

"Will what she tells the police be of any help?" he asked.

"It very well may be," I said vaguely.

What I did not tell him was that a deep sense of dread gnawed at my heart, a fear that we were far from seeing the end of any of this.

8

When we arrived back at Mrs. Montford's home, Mr. Jerome had changed his mind. Instead of going right to the authorities, he decided to come in with me to speak with his aunt.

It seemed that the trip in the car had somehow solidified his resolve on the matter and his trust in me had only deepened.

"I imagine my aunt will not be pleased that the matter has yet to be settled but at least she will be happy to be one step closer," Mr. Jerome said.

"Maybe so," I said as we made our way up the front steps. I was still far from convinced that anything Maddie might tell the police would be of use.

Mr. Fitzroy greeted us at the door and informed us

that Mrs. Montford was in the sunroom at the far end of the hall.

"Aunt Bea?" Mr. Jerome asked, the two of us walking into the room together. "Aunt Bea, are you in here?"

"Over here, boy."

I looked and found Mrs. Montford standing before the row of built-in shelves along the wall the door was fixed upon. It was filled with empty planter pots, all of which were ready to be filled for the spring. She seemed to be arranging them.

"Well, what did you learn?" she asked, dusting off her hands.

Mr. Jerome's eyes jumped to me at once. "Anna spoke with the maid," he said.

"I did, yes," I said.

"And?" Mrs. Montford asked, raising her brows as she looked at me. "What did she say?"

"She...told me a great deal," I said. "Things that she had been too frightened to tell anyone else."

Mrs. Montford's eyebrows rose even further. "Really?"

"Yes," I said. "And I have chosen to keep the girl's secrets, until she has the chance to speak with the police."

Her expression hardened. "Did she kill him?" she asked.

"I do not think so but I cannot yet be certain. I hope for her innocence," I said.

"Yet you keep her secrets," Mrs. Montford said, walking away from us and toward the sitting area nearer to the windows.

"She does not wish to endanger the girl," Mr. Jerome said, using my own words from earlier.

Mrs. Montford glanced at me, her eyes flashing. "Yes, well, she has agreed to speak with the police?"

"Yes, ma'am," I said.

"That is all there is to it then," she said, folding her hands. "They will do with her information what they will."

She took a seat at the window, picked up a cross stitch that was partially finished, and resumed working on it.

Mr. Jerome looked over at me, his eyes betraying surprise.

This is not the response we were expecting...

I had thought she would be a great deal more upset that there were no further answers. Given how we had spoken about the other deaths in detail, I thought she would immediately begin a barrage of questions for both her nephew and me. I had prepared myself for an assault that I might not be able to refuse.

"Well, then you must be on your way, Jerome," Mrs. Montford said. "I know it will not do you well to delay in sharing this information. Off you go."

"Very well," Mr. Jerome said. "Are you all right, Aunt?"

"Of course," she said tersely, glowering at him. "You do not want to delay."

"Right," he said. He turned to me. "Thank you, Anna. You were a great deal of help."

"I do not know that to be true," I said. "We still do not know who killed Mr. Finch."

"Perhaps not at this moment," he said. "But I hope that whatever it is Maddie has to tell the police will prove to be useful and give them new avenues to explore."

"I certainly hope so," I said.

He turned to leave.

"Mr. Jerome?" I said, suddenly.

He stopped and looked back at me. "Yes?"

"Thank you," I said. "For...understanding."

He studied me and then he gave a small smile. "You are quite welcome." He looked past me. "Rest up, my dear aunt. I shall see you soon."

"Thank you," she said with a small wave.

I watched him leave and then I looked back at Mrs. Montford.

"Now, girl," she said, examining her cross stitch without looking up at me. "Why don't you come sit with me?"

Sit with her? What did she mean? Why did she want me to sit with her?

"Come along," she said, finally looking at me.

I moved to the seat across from her and gingerly sat down.

"Now," she said, resuming her work. "I believe there is something that you are keeping from me."

I hesitated.

"Well?" she asked, glancing up at me over the top of the small, wooden hoop. "Are you hiding something?"

"What do you mean, ma'am?" I asked.

She pursed her lips. "Do not think me so foolish as to press you about what you learned from that housemaid," she said, her eyes lingering on the pattern she had begun with a bright red thread. "Though I could certainly do so and you would be obliged to tell me."

I tried to swallow but my throat was terribly dry. I coughed, sputtering slightly. "Yes, ma'am," I managed to murmur.

"However, I will not," she said. "Not unless that information becomes necessary. What I mean is that you have been rather preoccupied since you went back to that orphanage."

Color appeared in my cheeks. "Mrs. Montford, I am not keeping anything from you," I said. "Nothing of importance."

She looked up, her eyes narrowing slightly, her expression blank. "I did not think it would be anything that would cause harm to me but I am concerned about what has you so troubled."

It struck me how easily she had been able to see through me and my worries. Had I been that transparent? Had she learned my mannerisms well enough to be able to distinguish when I was troubled and when I was not?

Better yet, why did she care at all?

"Am I incorrect?" she pressed.

"N-No," I said, the skin of my palms growing slick with sweat. "I suppose...well, Mrs. Montford, I am not a great deal proud of what... And there is nothing I can do about—"

"Do not avoid the question, girl," she said, lowering the hoop slightly, her hand poised with the needle pressed between her thumb and forefinger. "Just answer it."

"I learned something of my past when I visited," I confessed. "Something that, in a way, I wish I had never learned at all."

"Oh?" she asked, pausing her sewing for a moment. "How so?"

I debated telling her how I found the information but that was not the part that troubled me. What I had learned was what mattered. "I learned...that I very likely have family in the city. My father's two sisters."

Mrs. Montford's eyes widened. "Truly?" she asked. "Well, that is interesting, isn't it?"

"Yes ,well..." I said. "I learned that they were in my father's will and had agreed to take me in if anything were to happen to him as it had to my mother. It seems that one of the Sisters at the orphanage had written to them several times and none of the letters were answered."

Mrs. Montford studied me but her face betrayed nothing. Perhaps it was being married to a man of the military for so many years but she had utterly perfected the ways of veiling her emotions. Even her eyes, sharp and clear as they were, revealed nothing.

"It seems that the police even went to one of their homes but they refused to speak on the matter," I said. "For some reason, their agreement with my father meant nothing to them, evidently."

"They would not visit you? Or the orphanage?" she asked.

I shook my head. "I never knew they existed. Not until I found out the other day."

She let out a sigh. "Good heavens, girl," she said, and then she gave me a small, sad smile.

My chest tightened and my eyes began to sting.

She is...sad, I realized. *Sad for me.*

"To learn that you have family who did not want you..." she said. "I am sorry, Anna. That must have been terribly difficult news to hear."

She set her sewing aside and looked at me pointedly. "There must be a great deal on your mind. You must have many questions."

"I certainly do," I said.

Something changed in her gaze. It softened and she regarded me with a kindness that I had only seen one other time...the night that the Colonel died.

In that moment we were two women, sitting together in the sunroom in the late afternoon. She shared my concerns and I shared hers. We might almost have been friends, rather than a lady and her servant.

It *felt* different. The expectations and responsibilities between the two of us had been temporarily suspended and together we were simply people without status or means. I spoke, she listened. It was as simple as that and yet, at the same time, as complicated.

"Well," she said. "I wish there was some way to encourage you. I am sorry you had to find out the way you did, instead of the women honoring their word to your father and coming to retrieve you when they should have."

"Thank you," I said. "You are very kind, ma'am."

And just like that, we resumed our respective roles once more.

She glanced over my shoulder at the clock on the shelf. "Good gracious," she said, getting to her feet. "I must hurry or I will be late for my fitting."

I rose with her. "May I fetch anything for you, ma'am? Your hat? Gloves, perhaps?"

"Yes, do," she said. "I shall meet you in the foyer."

I hurried from the room and took to the stairs.

As I went up, I thought of the way she had addressed my concerns. It was very unlike her to ask about the state of my feelings.

Having crossed over the threshold of her room, a sudden jolt of disappointment spread through me as the truth came to me.

Her questions were not a courtesy, I realized as I stared at some vague, distant spot on the opposite wall. *They were a distraction from the news that Mr. Jerome and I brought.*

The timing had been strange indeed, I thought as I hurried for the gloves and hat resting atop her dresser drawers.

I had thought it somewhat strange, the way she had chased Mr. Jerome from the sunroom, but as she changed the conversation around to me, I had almost forgotten about it entirely. It was not a simple shift in conversation, either. She asked me personal, deep questions.

Why? Only to forget her own troubles for a few moments? Or was there some other reason for her desire not to speak of Mr. Finch?

It was hard to know.

I retrieved her hat and gloves and started back down the stairs.

Why would she want to redirect the conversation so quickly? I wondered. *Could she possibly be hiding something about Mr. Finch's death?*

9

As I sat alongside Mrs. Montford in the car on the way downtown to the seamstress, I realized that I could not ignore the thought that Mrs. Montford was now hiding something. I had never seen her act as she had with Mr. Jerome. It was not as if I had never seen her dismissive but she seemed...almost desperate.

We arrived at the seamstress's shop a short time later, after a rather uncomfortable and almost silent ride. Mrs. Montford seemed oblivious to my inner turmoil, which I realized might very well be incorrect, given how easily she had noticed my frustration with what had transpired at the orphanage. It made me wonder if she paid greater attention to me than I realized and if she knew me better than I thought she did.

I followed her into the seamstress's shop, which sat

at the corner of a quaint street that was not far from the Thames. It was a part of town that I had not yet visited and that made me realize that, as large as the city was, I might never see every inch of it.

The room smelled of potpourri. Purple velvet curtains ran up and down the length of the walls, hiding them from view. Several dressing screens were lined up along one wall, creating areas which woman disappeared behind, the curtains further concealing them.

A rather boisterous woman prowled up and down along the room, energetically waving a large feather plume in her hand, as if it were a fan.

"Yes, of course, Mrs. Valerie. Don't you look *lovely*?" she would say to one customer, before rushing on to converse with the next.

She turned at the sound of the bell chiming in the door and gave a dramatic gasp.

"*Beatrice?*"

"Hello, Eleanor," Mrs. Montford said.

The woman named Eleanor hurried over to us, her large eyes round. "Good heavens, I was quite convinced you would never return to London," she said, with a sweeping wave of her arm, which she threw around Mrs. Montford's shoulders. "Oh, how *wonderful* it is to see you again, darling."

"I am pleased to see you as well," Mrs. Montford said, though her tight smile told me otherwise.

Eleanor fluttered her long, spidery eyelashes. "Now, what brings you all the way down to my little shop, hmm?" she asked, almost preening like the peacock whose feather she must have made off with. "Are you here on holiday? Or have you come as a more permanent resident of our fine city?"

"I am here for the time being," Mrs. Montford said tactfully. "I was hoping you might be able to make up a dress for me."

"Well, *of course*," Eleanor said with another sweeping gesture toward the back wall, where I noticed for the first time a door painted the same shade of purple as the curtains. "Come with me and we shall discuss your new dress, shall we?"

I lagged behind them, looking out over the other customers who were busy with their own affairs. I watched a woman with long blonde tresses browse a row of mannequins all adorned in elegant gowns and dinner dresses. Another led a young attendant to one of the dressing areas, arms loaded with enough gowns to bury the poor girl.

I asked myself if Mrs. Montford had some other engagement that I was not yet aware of, a party that she planned to attend. I wondered if Mr. Jerome would be in attendance, which made me then wonder how his time with the police had gone.

Eleanor opened the door, which led into a handsomely decorated area. The walls, lined with reams of every color fabric I could imagine, made the space wonderfully alive and vibrant. There were several work tables strewn around the room where young women handled delicate silks and soft linen. I noticed a particularly pretty piece of blue wool, which a young girl no older than sixteen or seventeen held gently, hand stitching a rose upon it in bright red. I caught her eye as we walked past and she gave me a shy smile.

I returned it as Eleanor stepped up to a table near the wall and produced a thick book filled with what appeared to be scraps of fabric.

"Now, dear, what were you thinking?" she asked, flipping the book open and beginning to look through the swatches within. "How about a lovely lace dress? Perhaps over a pale satin?"

"That would be fine," Mrs. Montford said, stepping up to the table beside her.

"What is this gown for, dear?" Eleanor asked, flipping further to a selection of lace. "A dinner, perhaps? Or a military ball for the Colonel?" she gasped. "Of course we will have to make him a matching pocket square from the scraps—"

She stopped at the sight of Mrs. Montford's somber expression.

"Oh," she said, laying her hand over her heart. "Have I...been insensitive?"

Mrs. Montford hesitated. "The Colonel has passed away," she said. There was no need for further explanation. I could see she had little desire to share the full truth of what happened.

Eleanor's face fell. "Oh, Beatrice..." she said, gently placing her bony hand on my mistress's arm. "You poor, poor dear. When did this happen?"

"On his birthday, in October," Mrs. Montford said, a tightness to her words.

Eleanor shook her head. "I cannot believe it..." she murmured. "Please forgive me for being so thoughtless."'

"No, no," Mrs. Montford said. "How could you have known?"

"To be perfectly honest, I am rather surprised the news has not yet become more common knowledge," Eleanor said. Her eyes widened. "Especially since I have already heard, through some of my friends, that Mr. Finch was recently found dead. Is that true? Please tell me it is not true."

I looked up, sensing Mrs. Montford tensing beside me.

The color in her cheeks disappeared.

"It...is true," she said, though her voice held a twinge of...anger?

Eleanor's eyes widened even further, her mouth falling open. "Oh, it cannot *be!*" she said. "To lose not only your husband but such a dear old friend as well? Beatrice, you poor thing, you must be so terribly upset. What happened? How did he—"

Mrs. Montford reached up and laid her hand suddenly against her forehead. She swayed and had to grab the end of the table beside her.

I was at her side in a moment. "Mrs. Montford, are you all right?" I asked, holding my arms out to stop her lest she fell.

"Oh..." she breathed, her eyelids fluttering. "I-I do not know what came over me."

Eleanor's brow furrowed and she frowned at Mrs. Montford. "Please, you must sit down. Might I bring you some water?" She lifted a folder and began waving it in front of Mrs. Montford's face to create a breeze.

Mrs. Montford shook her head. "No...thank you."

She straightened, rubbing her forehead gently. Then, she looked over at me and some of the color returned to her cheeks.

"I...I am sorry, Eleanor, but I think I will have to reschedule," she said. "I am suddenly feeling quite weak."

"Of course, dear, of course," Eleanor said, nodding quickly. "No trouble at all. I would be happy to fit you in."

Mrs. Montford nodded and she turned and started toward the door.

I hurried to keep up with her. "Mrs. Montford, is there anything I can—"

"No," she snapped and started to move more quickly away.

I followed her out through the door and up to the waiting car. The driver seemed surprised to see us but at once went to open the door.

"Allow me to help," I began.

"Leave me be, girl," Mrs. Montford snapped, rounding on me, her jaw clenched.

She met my gaze and the anger flashing in her eyes caused me to take a full step back.

She swept into the car and it took me three heartbeats to consider following after her. I knew that I had no other way home but the sheer force of her reaction to a simple request of mine to help her had stunned me to utter silence.

I managed to find the courage to slide into the car beside her, the door promptly being closed behind me. I did not look at her and I hardly dared to breathe beside her lest she lash out at me once more.

It was not until we were well on our way, and nearly home, that I realized she certainly did not *seem* ill any longer. I had been so concerned at the shop that I had hardly stopped to think about her sudden change of demeanor.

It was strange, was it not? She had appeared faint in the shop but as soon as we stepped outside she became almost hostile.

As I considered it even further, I realized that the *timing* of her sudden illness had been the strangest of all. Had it not been just after Eleanor had mentioned Mr. Finch?

That seemed awfully strange, especially given my earlier suspicions that she had been intentionally avoiding speaking about Mr. Finch with her nephew after we had returned from speaking with Maddie.

It is entirely possible that she is hiding something.

The thought sent a shiver down my whole spine as the car slowed to a stop just outside the house.

What would she have to hide? And why?

I followed her up the front steps and into the house where Mr. Fitzroy greeted us. She seemed dismissive with the butler, as well.

As I passed by him, I mouthed a short, "Sorry..."

She started toward the stairs but rounded on me as I came up to her. "I have some letters that I must write," she announced. "I need you to go out and buy fresh ink. My fountain pens are all terribly low and I do not believe I have any remaining ink in my desk."

"Of course, ma'am," I said, inclining my head, although it seemed an odd request. I almost wondered if she was inventing an errand to be rid of me, so that I would not have time to notice her sudden recovery from her dizzy spell.

I did not speak the thought aloud, only saying, "Nothing would please me more."

"Very good," she said heavily. She turned and

started up the stairs. "I shall be in my room. Please leave the ink with Mr. Fitzroy when you return."

I watched her until she disappeared at the top of the landing.

I swallowed hard, my unease growing.

Mr. Finch's death had created a new sort of animosity in my mistress that I had never seen in my entire time serving her. A mark of her character had always been her ability to remain cool in difficult situations. Even when her own husband died, she had been more poised than she was now.

It could be explained away as her being overwhelmed with the sheer number of deaths that we have had to endure these past weeks, I thought. *That would be enough to change anyone, would it not?*

Regardless, I wondered if it was because of Mr. Finch himself being the victim. If that was true, what was it about *him* in particular that bothered her so much? How could his loss distress her more than her own husband's death?

As I turned toward the door, a ridiculous, wild thought flitted through my head.

Suppose she knows something about what happened to him, was even involved in his death in some way?

I tried to shake it, but once it had hold of me, the idea crashed against my mind like an icy wave slamming into the cliffs.

It was impossible, of course. Mrs. Montford was incapable of harming anyone...wasn't she?

I slipped behind the open door to the coat closet and leaned back against the wall, bathed in shadow.

My heart raced with this new suspicion but I shook my head.

I am allowing my emotions to get away from me, I thought, trying to say it as loudly and as clearly in my mind as I could. *It is a foolish thought and I should kill it here and now before I am unable to get rid of it.*

I straightened and balled my hands into fists.

I was finding ghosts and shadows where there were none. That was all.

Remembering my errand, I decided the best thing to do was to check and see if there were any ink refills in storage that Mrs. Montford might be able to use while I went shopping for her. The best person to ask would be the housekeeper, Mrs. Carlisle.

I found her in the dining room arranging Mrs. Montford's place at the table. Upon first glance, it seemed that she had chosen Mrs. Montford's mother's blue china, a set that she kept back for occasional use, typically when guests were expected.

I paused before I entered.

Mrs. Carlisle had been working for the Montfords for many years. Almost her entire career had been spent at Mrs. Montford's side. As head housekeeper, she had full rule of the house and certainly knew a great deal of the goings on. She would know things about our employer that even I was not privy to.

Perhaps she could have some answers about my mistress's friendship with Mr. Finch.

I did not wish to press Mrs. Carlisle, though, knowing that one step out of line would surely make her suspicious about my purpose.

"Good afternoon, Mrs. Carlisle," I said, stepping into the room.

"Good afternoon," she said, glancing briefly at me before returning to arranging the plating before her. It would normally have been the butler's task to oversee such details but Mrs. Carlisle, I knew, was most particular about the table settings and preferred to check them herself.

"I had hoped to find you," I said. "I was wondering if you would know of any extra ink that might be in storage? Mrs. Montford is in need."

Mrs. Carlisle looked up, her eyebrow arching, her expression cool. "Is that what has upset her so terribly?" she asked.

My heart sank. "What do you mean?"

"I heard the way she snapped at you before she went upstairs," she said. "The look on her face was quite clear."

I had not thought she had snapped at me, at least not the way she had before we had left the seamstress. Perhaps I had grown used to the way she spoke to me and did not consider that to be a sign of distress.

"What did you do to trouble her?" Mrs. Carlisle asked.

My face burned. She acted as if it was a regular occurrence. "I do not think it was I that upset her," I said. "Something else is troubling her and I cannot quite place what it is."

Mrs. Carlisle's nostrils flared as she surveyed the place setting before her and reached out to shift the outer piece of cutlery ever so slightly to the left, straightening it. "Yes, I suppose I have noticed a change in her usual attitude."

That pleased me to hear, knowing that I was not the only one. "Do you have any idea what it might be?" I asked.

She glared at me. "I had hoped you might be able to answer that," she said. "You are with her all the time, aren't you?"

"Yes," I said. "But all I know is that she seems almost more disturbed than when the Colonel died."

Mrs. Carlisle pursed her lips, her chin still lifted high. "Hmm..." she murmured. "I have to admit that I agree."

I knew that I had to move carefully. Mrs. Montford would be none too pleased to hear that I had been asking questions, which she might consider to be gossiping about her.

"I have wondered if it might have anything at all to do with...Mr. Finch," I said, chancing it.

Mrs. Carlisle's hand delicately moved the crystal flute ever so slightly. She did not look up at me. "What makes you think that?"

"The timing," I said. "She has been not quite herself since the night of his death."

The housekeeper's eyebrows rose. "Well, I suppose I can hardly blame her," she said. Her eyes became suddenly distant. "Given the fact that the Montfords, Mr. Finch, Major Lewis, and the Townsons were all very good friends for many years. Good heavens, it was a long time."

I watched her, curious now. "They all were friends for that long?" I asked.

"Yes," she said. "Mr. Finch and the Colonel were very good friends. They spent a great deal of time together whenever Mrs. Montford and the Colonel were in London."

"What happened?" I asked. "In all my time working for her, I have not known some of these people."

Mrs. Carlisle became herself again, grabbing the box resting on Mrs. Montford's chair, which was filled with another full set of dishes. "I hardly know," she said. "It is not my business knowing why or why not Mrs. Montford and the Colonel might have chosen to no longer engage socially with their London friends."

She walked around to the other side of the table

and set the box down to begin unloading it. She sighed and paused.

"Though I suppose the real reason is that when they stopped coming to town, they simply drifted apart," she said. Then, she glared at me. "Do not suppose that there is some nefarious reason."

"I would never suggest it," I said, though at once I wondered why she had worded it in such a way.

Mrs. Carlisle looked at me once more and glowered. "Did Mrs. Montford not send you away for some ink? You should not delay a moment longer."

"Yes, of course," I said, turning to leave the room. "Though you never answered my question about whether we have any stored ink that I might give her in the meantime."

"No," Mrs. Carlisle snapped. "Now get going."

With a sniff, she turned and left the room, stepping back into the kitchen.

I stared after her, my brow furrowing.

First Mrs. Montford and now Mrs. Carlisle acting so irritably, I thought. *And all because of this Mr. Finch.*

I became all the more convinced that Mrs. Montford, and now Mrs. Carlisle, was hiding something. There was a piece to this puzzle that I did not know.

Mrs. Carlisle confirming their longstanding friendship further explained Mrs. Montford's cautious yet relatively pleased greeting with Mr. Finch at Mrs. Townson's party.

Still, it did make me wonder what it was that the two women knew and had no interest in sharing with me. I wondered if I should have pressed the housekeeper further but quickly realized that she would not have shared anything else. She was loyally protecting Mrs. Montford.

The question is, from what?

10

I did not linger any longer than I needed to at the house, knowing it would not do to upset Mrs. Montford any further. I did not wish to cross paths with Mrs. Carlisle again, either, knowing that she would likely chase me away without a great deal of kindness.

As I stepped outside, a shiver rushed down my spine and I pulled my gloves from my pockets. The January chill filled the air, both with its grey skies and biting cold. The wind brushed against the exposed skin of my face, before I tugged my scarf higher to protect it.

I started down the street toward the shops, dodging a woman walking her small dog and apologizing as I did so, yet my mind was elsewhere.

The shop that Mrs. Montford preferred was at the

end of a long stretch of them, four blocks away. The street where Mr. Ronald's General Goods was located was wide and open, stretching directly from east to west. Mr. Ronald's shop was near the middle, between a grocer and a butcher. The large windows housed some of the goods he had for sale, including pieces of furniture, books, candlesticks, crockery, and many other things tastefully arranged to lure the passersby inside.

I opened the door and a rush of warm air passed over me. I breathed it in, the heady scent of charred wood and smoke greeting me like an old friend. As I pulled the door closed, a bell chimed, alerting those within of my presence.

The store had been rearranged since I was in last. Where a set of lamps and a crate stacked with rolled rugs had once been, there was now a long table filled with scarves, hats, and gloves, along with an open trunk of boots, all ready for winter use.

I stepped up to the table briefly to examine the clothing upon it. I glanced at the fingertips of my own gloves as I removed them and knew it was likely that they would need to be replaced soon. Before I had the chance to decide if I had enough money tucked away back home, approaching footsteps drew my attention away.

I looked up to see a thin, tall man who reminded me a great deal of a scarecrow approaching. He had a kind smile and eyes that reminded me of a friendly dog.

"Good afternoon," he said. His eyes widened slightly as recognition glinted within them. "Ah, you are here for Mrs. Montford. Am I right?"

"Yes," I said. "She has sent me out for ink to refill her fountain pens."

"Well, certainly," he said, his easy smile growing. He turned and waved for me to follow as he lumbered along between the tables of goods toward the back wall. "How is Mrs. Montford?"

"Very well, sir," I said, following after.

"Good, good," Mr. Ronald said, taking a turn at a shelf of planter pots. I went after him and found him standing before a shelf stacked high with bundles of paper tied with string, along with a few boxes of different colored pens, and a row of various sizes of ink bottles.

"Here we are," he said.

"Thank you, sir."

As I reached out to select a bottle, I realized I had not asked after precisely what sort of ink my mistress would want.

"Is everything all right?" Mr. Ronald asked.

I looked up at him. "You would not, by any chance, know what sort of ink my lady usually prefers?" I asked.

He nodded. "Of course, I have a record of many of

my regular customers' purchases. I keep it back at the counter. If you follow me, I can find that record for you."

"Thank you. I would very much appreciate it," I said.

He nodded and led me to a long, four-sided wooden counter that ran through the middle of the shop, a perfect square amidst all the tables, boxes, and shelves. He lifted a flap along the back and slipped beneath it.

Humming a merry little tune, he ducked down behind the counter and produced a stack of leather-bound books. He rifled through the stack and picked one from the bottom.

"I believe it is in here," he said.

He laid the book down and flipped it open, then looked up at me. "I have heard Colonel Montford passed away. Is that true? Or simply gossip?"

I tried to swallow but my throat had gone dry. "Yes," I said. "Back before Christmas."

Mr. Ronald let out an exaggerated sigh. "How tragic," he said, shaking his head as he began to turn the pages of what I now realized to be a log book. "I had hoped it was nothing more than rumor."

He paused, eyes sweeping over the names at the top.

"How has Mrs. Montford been dealing with her sad

loss?" he asked, flipping further toward the back of the book.

Despite his disapproving tone when he had spoken of rumor and gossip, I sensed he secretly hoped for a harmless little piece of either to add some interest to his day.

"It has been trying," I said cautiously, uncertain how much Mrs. Montford would want me to share of her personal life. "She does miss him a great deal."

"Was it sudden?" Mr. Ronald asked, pausing briefly to look at me.

"Yes," I said and left it at that.

He nodded. "I see."

He continued to look through the pages and then paused again.

"And how is she with the death of Mr. Finch? I believe he was a friend to the Montford family?"

The question startled me, as it caught me off guard that he would make that connection so quickly. I had known Mrs. Montford and the late Colonel were friends with Mr. Finch but it surprised me to see how many others, even casual acquaintances and shop-keepers, had known of that. It reminded me once more that Mrs. Montford had a long history and a long life prior to me entering into it. There was still a great deal that I did not know about her or her past and likely a great deal that I would simply never know.

"As one might imagine, she has had to endure a great deal as of late," I said. "It has been difficult."

Mr. Ronald shook his head. "To lose her husband and a friend..." he said. "I knew Mr. Finch myself. It shocked me when I learned of his death."

My ears perked up. "I am sorry to hear that," I said.

He gave me a small smile in return, any sadness he may have felt clearly not enough to remove his eagerness for conversation. "He was a business colleague. We saw one another often and became well acquainted."

It struck me as interesting that the shopkeeper would know someone whom Mr. Jerome had described as a businessman of sorts. Perhaps Mr. Finch had needed supplies and purchased them from Mr. Ronald.

"I, for one, will miss his handiwork," Mr. Ronald said, flipping back to the front page to check the names listed on the page. "Leatherwork is a rare trade these days and if I ever needed anything repaired, I knew that I could count on him."

"I thought he provided items primarily for the military," I said, my brow furrowing.

"Oh, yes, he did," Mr. Ronald said. "He made rifle slings, quite specialized and typically reserved for officers, used especially for ceremonies and formal occasions." He tapped the page with the end of his finger and I briefly caught sight of *Colonel Montford* before he slipped his hand halfway through the book and began his search once more. "Mr. Finch was quite the sales-man, though it might have gotten him into trouble a time or two."

Gotten him into trouble?

This was the first time I had heard anything nega-tive about the deceased. Mr. Jerome had said only good things and others had spoken highly of him as well.

Then again, is that entirely true? I wondered. I had heard a few people mention the man was a good friend but what else was there to his character? Did I truly know anything?

Luckily, if I wanted information, it seemed I had come to the right place.

"Yes, as good as his quality of work was, his craft was not what drove him," Mr. Ronald went on, procuring a pair of spectacles from the pocket of his shirt. "Ah, yes, here we are...Montford, Montford... The ink, yes...which one?"

"What do you mean when you say Mr. Finch's work was not what drove him?" I prompted. "What did moti-vate him, then?"

He looked up at me, his eyes three times their usual size through the thick lenses of his spectacles. "Money, of course. He was always more interested in acquiring wealth than anything else."

Money, I thought. There might never have been a better motive for murdering someone. Greed was the pure antithesis of good character. It robbed men of their sense and destroyed lives.

"I must say he charged an exorbitant amount for his goods," Mr. Ronald said. "Some would say it was not worth what he asked and demanded that he trade more fairly. He, however, had little regard for his own clientele. He would do business with anyone willing to pay, which many of his friends warned him could lead to bad things."

His friends. I wondered if the Colonel or Mrs. Montford had been among those.

"Do you mean that he would sell to unsavory sorts?" I asked.

He nodded. "Yes, certainly," he said. "Ah! Here we are. Yes, the Colonel's preferred ink was always the Avery brand in black."

I nodded. "I see," I said. "Thank you, Mr. Ronald."

He closed the book. "Of course," he said. "And as for Mr. Finch, it is rather sad what happened to him. I do hope that he did not make some deal that got him into trouble."

A *deal gone bad,* I thought. Just as I had thought. Greed.

I did wonder what sort of clientele Mr. Ronald was referring to but more customers had entered the shop and I sensed he would be less willing to gossip before an audience. "Thank you again, Mr. Ronald. Mrs. Montford will be pleased."

I left him the money I would need to pay before I went back to grab a few of the bottles.

I tucked them away in the satchel I had brought with me and made my way toward the door.

As I walked back to Mrs. Montford's, the ink packed safely away, I considered what the shopkeeper had said.

It seemed that Mr. Finch was respected and popular, at least enough so that his name was known, not only in the circles Mrs. Montford moved in, but among the local tradesmen as well. According to Mr. Ronald, he was also a bit greedy.

I then considered the dead man's relationship with my mistress and tried to make sense of the way she had been acting since his death. She had greeted him the night of the party in a somewhat cool manner but I had since learned what close friends they had been. His death had struck her but she seemed to be hiding something about it. Something about the deceased himself, most likely.

What was it? What was she so frightened of anyone seeing? It was as if she wanted nothing more than for the whole matter to simply disappear.

It seemed contrary to her character. With every other death that we had so unfortunately experienced in the past, she had wanted to see answers discovered and those responsible for the killings brought to justice. Yet this time, she seemed...entirely different.

She had washed her hands of it and of Mr.
Finch. Why?

It was particularly odd because of how Mr. Jerome
saw the whole affair. He wanted to find the truth, as the
murder had occurred beneath the roof of his family
home. Now, it was his aunt who did not want to be
involved.

*So what is it that Mrs. Montford knows? Why is she
behaving the way she is?*

I had many questions, and for the first time, I felt as
if Mrs. Montford and I were on opposing sides. Why
did it trouble me so much that she was hiding things
from me now? I knew for certain that she must have
kept many things from me before. Why was it so both-
ersome in this situation?

As I approached the house, a troubling thought
returned to my mind.

*What if Mrs. Montford does not want to discuss the
matter because she is protecting the person responsible? She
could even be that person herself.*

It was impossible, of course. Outrageous. But now
that I'd had the thought, I could not seem to shake it.

I knew that I must let it go. The idea was absurd.
Bordering insanity.

But could it be true, all the same?

11

Mercifully, Mrs. Montford did not wish to see me for the majority of the rest of the day. That, at least, saved me the effort of trying to behave in an ordinary way around her, as if I had never had the thought that she could be a murderer.

Upon my return with her fresh bottles of ink, she accepted them and then sent me on my way. I spent the rest of the afternoon tidying up my room and listening to questions from Selina, who seemed to notice that I was acting awfully strange. She also wondered why Mrs. Montford had been so cross earlier.

"Did something happen at the seamstress's?" she asked, hovering just outside my door.

"Well...yes," I said, keeping my voice low. I told her

about how Mr. Finch had been mentioned. "And she seemed to feign illness. It was the strangest thing."

Selina's brow furrowed and she crossed her arms, leaning against the doorframe. "That is odd," she said. "Do you suppose she acted that way as a means of escaping the conversation?"

"That is what I feared," I said. "Well, certainly, I worried that she was all right, first and foremost. But then when we stepped out to the car to leave, she snapped at me. At once I knew that it had been nothing more than a show."

Selina frowned. "That does seem strange."

"There must be some reason that Mr. Finch's death troubles her so," I said.

Selina's eyes narrowed. "You look as if you know something."

"Why do you think that?" I asked, trying to sound innocent.

She rolled her eyes. "Do you truly think lying will solve anything? And to me? As long as we've known one another, Anna, I can read you like a book."

I dropped the pretense. "I'm not trying to be sneaky. I simply do not know if the information I have is of any value."

"Well, then, out with it," she said with a snap of her fingers.

I hesitated. "Mr. Ronald down at the shop said Mr. Finch had some rather unsavory business partners."

Selina's eyes widened. "Oh," she said. "And the Colonel and Mrs. Montford were quite good friends with the man."

"Indeed," I said. "Mr. Ronald also said that Mr. Finch's friends often tried to tell him off for how he seemed to care little for the quality of his clientele."

"Perhaps Mrs. Montford knows something of his dealings?" Selina suggested.

"That is what I wonder as well," I said, dropping my voice even further. "She is hiding something, of that much I am certain."

Selina looked thoughtful. "I wonder what it could be."

"I can only imagine," I said. "And for some reason, nothing I imagine is good."

At that moment, a rather rambunctious pair of young scullery maids came tearing down the hall toward their quarters, being chased by one of the kitchen hands. Selina promptly went after them, threatening them all with the wooden spoons that Mrs. Rose kept solely for problematic kitchen crew.

I took the opportunity to disappear into my room. For some reason, discussing my distrust of Mrs. Montford made me feel disloyal and uncomfortable, even when it was only Selina I was confiding in.

Morning came without great excitement. I made my way to Mrs. Montford's room with a little apprehension, but she greeted me and the morning with a warmth that I had not seen in some time.

As I brushed her hair, doing my best not to make eye contact with her in the mirror, she said, "I regret being short with you yesterday, Anna. I had a great deal on my mind."

I knew it was the closest thing to an apology I was likely to get and it eased my mind slightly. It seemed that the air between us had been cleared.

Her momentary slip in composure had righted itself and she returned to her usual behavior as we made our way down for breakfast.

While she had her favorite eggs with ham, I hovered near the side table, ready to refill anything she might need.

"Mr. Jerome Townson, ma'am," the butler announced.

The clink of silverware prefaced her looking up. She dabbed at her mouth with her napkin. "See him in."

Just as he had a few mornings before, Mr. Jerome slipped into the room. His eyes swept the room and he first smiled at his aunt before catching my own gaze.

I was pleased that he moved at once to take the seat beside his aunt, as it ensured that he did not see my cheeks turning pink.

"Perhaps we should begin setting a place for you at

breakfast time," Mrs. Montford said with a lifted eyebrow, as he leaned against the table.

"Perhaps you should," he said with a grin. "I do not mean to disturb you so early but I did come with some news. Have you received the post yet?"

"No," Mrs. Montford said. "Mr. Fitzroy typically brings it to me whilst I have my breakfast."

Mr. Jerome did not hesitate to get to his feet and head right back out through the door.

The crackle of the burning logs in the fireplace was all we heard for a few long moments as we waited for his return.

He did return, with Mr. Fitzroy.

"Just as I thought," Mr. Jerome said, holding an envelope in his hand. "I had hoped to speak with you about this."

"What is it?" Mrs. Montford asked, stretching out her hand.

Mr. Jerome passed it to her and resumed his seat.

"An invitation," he said. "From Major Lewis."

Mrs. Montford's brow furrowed. She took a knife from the table and slit the envelope open.

Mr. Fitzroy watched her warily from near the door with the same apprehension on his face that I felt. Major Lewis? Did this have something to do with Mr. Finch's death?

"A memorial dinner?" Mrs. Montford asked,

looking up at her nephew over the top of the invitation.

"Yes," Mr. Jerome said. "From what you can see in the invitation, he hopes that we can all gather together to honor your late friend."

Mrs. Montford stiffened and dropped the invitation as if it had stung her.

"It's all right," Mr. Jerome said. "You do not need to be frightened, Aunt."

"I am not frightened," she said, glaring at him. "But that does not mean that I wish to go and glorify his death."

"It is not meant to be that way," Mr. Jerome said. "No, it is meant to be a celebration."

Mrs. Montford frowned at him. "What are we meant to celebrate when the reason for his death has not yet been discovered? Is it not disrespectful?"

Mr. Jerome's eyes narrowed. "Aunt, what is this about?" he asked. "You have been acting so strangely ever since—"

"I have done no such thing," she said sharply.

I stared at her. She reminded me of a petulant child who had been caught misbehaving. At the same time, it surprised me to hear her nephew so openly confronting her.

"Well, there was an additional note for me in my invitation," Mr. Jerome said. "Which is why I am here in the first place."

"Oh?" she asked, folding her arms. She appeared reluctant to hear anything else from him.

"He seemed certain that out of everyone he invited, you would be the only one to consider not coming," Mr. Jerome said.

Mrs. Montford gaped at him, her eyes widening, her stubborn expression fading. "Me?" she asked. "Why would he—"

"He said that you would say precisely what you just did," Mr. Jerome said. "That the matter has not yet been resolved and you would be concerned about that."

She clucked her tongue and folded her arms.

"That being the case, he asked me to see you and try to convince you to come tonight."

"Why?" she asked.

"Because it is important for all of you to be together right now, as friends," Mr. Jerome said. "He wants to honor the life of a man lost too soon. Do you not owe Mr. Finch that much?"

"I do not owe him anything," Mrs. Montford said.

"Was he not your friend?" Mr. Jerome asked.

She hesitated, her eyebrows high but her lips pressed tightly together. "He was," she said after a few moments but it almost seemed to pain her to admit as much.

"Then why would you not want to gather with your old friends this evening for a meal, as a way to remember the deceased?" Mr. Jerome asked. "That is all the Major is suggesting."

Mrs. Montford let out a long sigh. "Very well," she said. "I suppose I have little choice, do I?"

"Why are you so resistant?" her nephew asked. "It makes no sense to me."

"I am not resistant," she snapped, glowering at him.

He sighed, shaking his head.

I could understand his frustration. It was the same way I had been feeling about the matter as well. It appeared I was not the only one to think Mrs. Montford's behavior about this whole thing was...curious.

He glanced at me as if my thoughts had been voiced. For a moment, I felt the heat in my face crawl down my neck in fear that perhaps I had, in fact, spoken aloud.

"I only ask because...well, you must understand how troubling this has been for my mother," he said. "Since the death, she has not been able to sleep. She is becoming terribly paranoid about everything and everyone. She fears that the person responsible was one of her guests, one of her friends..."

Mrs. Montfort shifted in her seat.

"But I cannot imagine anything of the kind," he said. "I do not believe anyone in attendance that night was capable of such violence. You two, mother and I, Mr. and Mrs. Newton, Major Lewis..." He listed them all on his fingers as he spoke. "Mr. Finch, Lady Fitzwilliam—"

"What is your point?" Mrs. Montford asked.

He blinked at her. "I do not believe that my mother will be able to rest until she faces you all once more," he said. "This dinner, I believe, is Major Lewis's way of helping everyone come to terms with what happened and find a way to move past it."

Mrs. Montford frowned.

"I realize that it seems a bit morbid," he said. "But I do not think it will be at all like a funeral. As you read, it is meant to be a celebration of life."

He gave his aunt a keen look.

"Can you not do this? For the wellbeing of all?"

Mrs. Montford looked down at the invitation once more and slowly, ever so slowly, picked it up again. She read it a second time and let out a long sigh.

"You are right," she said. "The Major and everyone else are trying to make the best of a tragic situation. I can do no less."

My heart lightened. Perhaps she was beginning to come around. Maybe she had finally worked through whatever it was that had been ailing her.

"I shall go," she said. "But I do hope that the culprit is found. Have you heard nothing?"

"No," he said, shaking his head. "All the staff have been interrogated and the police are now quite certain that it was not any of them."

I wonder if they have spoken with Maddie by now, I thought.

Mrs. Montford hung her head, suddenly morose once more.

"Do not worry, Aunt Bea," Mr. Jerome said, laying a hand on her shoulder. "I realize tonight may be difficult but I think it will do us all good."

12

It was not long after Mr. Jerome left that Mrs. Montford began to speak as though she regretted agreeing to attend the party.

"Really, what is the point?" she asked as I selected a few dresses from her wardrobe. She sat in her favorite yellow armchair near the window, staring out at the dreary grey sky. "What are we to discuss, hmm? How fond we were of our old friend? How much he meant to us all?"

I tried my best to keep my expression blank as I selected a pretty grey dress from her collection. I thought black might have too many negative associations and push her even further away.

"It is going to be positively awful," she said, folding her arms. "I do not think I should go. They can all discuss Mr. Finch without me."

I pretended not to hear, as I selected another dress, this one bottle green, from her wardrobe.

"Though the Major would be disappointed," she mused. "I know that he would be over here first thing in the morning to check on me. Then I should have to endure hearing of the night's events all the same."

I turned to her jewelry box and pulled open the top drawer to find her collection of jewels and broaches. I chose a pretty dove carrying a branch speckled with tiny emeralds—a gift from the Colonel for their twentieth anniversary.

On second thought...

"I suppose I have no choice, then, do I?" she asked. "I must go."

I sighed, relieved. *Well, at least she realizes it is in her best interests.*

I hoped she would go, more than anything so that she would find some peace. Mr. Finch's death had taken a great toll on her. I knew she would need as much help from those closest to her as she could have. With the Colonel gone, her friends and their comfort would have to suffice. Mr. Jerome would help, certainly, but it was clear from his conversation that morning that his care was fixed squarely upon his mother, as it should be.

I did hope that the authorities would find whoever it was that was responsible and they would have to answer for the crime they had committed. I thought back to Mr. Ronald. His statement about Mr. Finch's unsavory clientele stuck with me. Had that played into his death?

It was not long before Mrs. Montford announced herself ready to leave. She had disregarded the broach I had set upon her dresser before leaving the room and I took it as a clear statement that she was either not yet ready to wear it or she wanted nothing to do with the memory of her late husband that evening.

She insisted I accompany her and I did not dare question it, lest she change her mind about going altogether. I knew her nephew and the others would be disappointed if she failed to make an appearance.

MR. JEROME WAS, in fact, quite pleased to see his aunt and I enter the parlor at Major Lewis's house. He approached us and greeted his aunt.

As she moved past him to speak with the other guests, he stepped up to me.

"I suppose I have you to thank for convincing her to come this evening," he said in a low voice.

"Not at all," I said. "She came of her own volition after you spoke with her this morning."

He looked unconvinced. "Maybe. But I sometimes suspect she listens to you more than to me," he said. "You have more influence than you realize."

I watched Mrs. Montford make her way toward Mrs. Townson, her expression softening as she smiled at everyone.

Footsteps behind us caused Mr. Jerome to turn. I followed suit to find Major Lewis coming through the doorway.

"Ah, good evening, good evening," he said with a broad grin across his handsome face. He walked over to Mr. Jerome and rested a hand on his shoulder. "I am so pleased that you were able to come." His gaze shifted to me. "And from your presence, Miss, I would say that Mrs. Montford is here?"

"She is," Mr. Jerome said with a nod. "It took a bit of convincing but she came around."

"Very good," our host said, looking out over the rest of the guests.

Everyone had gathered around the fireplace along the back wall, nearer to the bright orange flames that filled the room with their flickering, comforting light. The chill of the night invited the closeness.

I was pleased to see Mrs. Montford engaging with her friends when she had seemed so resistant earlier.

"Might I have you to thank for convincing her?" Major Lewis asked. It took me a moment to realize that he was speaking to me.

I said, "Actually, Mr. Townson is responsible."

"Well, thank you," Major Lewis said. "I wanted nothing more than for all of us to be together again.

That night was so terribly ruined. I realize nothing can ever change what happened but we cannot let our enemies win, can we?"

His expression grew even more serious. "I do wish that we could have had some answers by now, don't you? As far as I know, the police have not yet caught the killer."

Mr. Jerome's face fell. "Yes, they are still at a loss as to what happened," he said. "The only evidence they were able to find was the statue that was used to kill him. My mother could not bear to look at it or its partners any longer. She asked the servants to take them all and get rid of them. I was thankful I was home, as I was able to intercept them and simply have the lions put away for the time being."

"How tragic," Major Lewis said. "Your father was quite fond of those, wasn't he? And if I remember correctly, the one that was used to kill Mr. Finch was his favorite, was it not? The lion standing on the rock, proud and on the hunt?"

"Yes," Mr. Jerome said. I saw his brow furrow for a brief moment.

A bell sounded from somewhere further in the house.

Major Lewis brightened. "Ah, it sounds like dinner is served."

He raised his hands and clapped them a few times together.

"Everyone? Everyone! Dinner is now ready for us. If you would all be so kind as to join me in the dining room?"

He turned and left the room.

Mr. Jerome gave me a sidelong look and opened his mouth to speak but evidently decided against it.

I did not dare ask what it was he wanted to say, as Mrs. Montford came near. We all started down the hall toward the dining room.

The Major's home was larger than Mrs. Montford's and it was filled with what I could only assume to be memorabilia from his time in the army. The surfaces were uncluttered and gleaming as if polished right before our arrival. Every piece of furniture was in line, as pristine as if they were in a museum exhibit.

Seeing the lack of warmth that a woman's touch would often bring to a home made me wonder why the Major was not married. I tucked away the question to ask Mr. Jerome, if the opportunity ever presented itself, as we entered the dining room.

"Come in, come in," Major Lewis said from the head of the table. "Seat yourselves wherever you would like. We are all friends here and tonight is not about social standing. We are here to celebrate the life of our friend. I want this to be an occasion we all remember."

Mr. Jerome walked with his mother to the table and Mrs. Montford joined him on his other side.

I stayed near the wall along with two other servants who had accompanied their employers. I recognized one maid from Lady Fitzwilliam's home but she seemed as timid as a mouse, and as such, did everything she could to keep her eyes fixed on her own shoes.

As servers brought drinks and a first course to the table, conversation among the guests became consistent and comfortable. I heard snatches, from the weather to business and the gatherings around Christmas and looking ahead into the new year.

In a way, the night seemed to have picked up right where the last had ended, apart from Mr. Finch's absence, which for the time being, seemed to go unnoticed.

*No, not unnoticed...*I thought. It was the unacknowledged fact that hung in the air above our heads. In truth, I was quite certain that everyone was doing everything they could *not* to speak of him and to keep the focus of their conversations away from anything relating to him.

It startled me to realize that truth and at the same time it was rather sad.

The attempts to avoid speaking of him said more than any words ever could.

It was not until the third course was delivered that Major Lewis got to his feet, clinking the side of his glass with the edge of his spoon.

"May I have your attention, everyone? Yes, thank you," he said as the room fell silent around him.

He surveyed the guests with a sad smile.

"First of all, I would like to thank each of you for coming this evening," he said. "I realize that it might have been difficult to accept my invitation, knowing the precise reason for the evening."

Mrs. Townson glanced sidelong at her son. I noticed Lady Fitzwilliam look up and meet what I could only imagine to be Mrs. Montford's gaze.

"Yes, we are here this evening to honor the life of our late friend, Mr. Finch," Major Lewis said, his back straightening, his brow furrowing. I almost expected him to salute, as it seemed he was honoring a fallen soldier or some such.

A heavy silence pressed in around us and the warmth of the candles and the laughter that had so recently filled the room seemed a distant memory.

"I shall make a toast," Major Lewis said, gesturing with the glass in his hand. "But first, I will ask if anyone would like to say a few words in honor of his life?"

One gentleman cleared his throat and his wife shifted beside him.

Neither Mr. Jerome nor his mother moved. Mrs. Montford looked down.

"Well, then I shall go first," Major Lewis said. "I, for one, must admit that I shall miss Mr. Finch's sense of humor. He always had a tale to tell of some sale he had made and we all know the colorful clients that he had."

Colorful? I thought. A kind way of saying questionable?

A low rumble of laughter passed through the guests and some of the morose expressions faded into gentler ones.

Mr. Jerome looked over at his mother, who straightened the utensils beside her plate into perfect rows beside one another.

"I shall miss his compassion," Mrs. Townson said suddenly, looking up from her silverware. "He had great love for those in need. I remember... I remember after Mr. Townson passed away, he came to check on me two or three times a week for the first few months, just to see if there was anything around the house my husband would have done that I might have needed help with."

Murmurs of agreement and recollection grew among the guests.

"Yes indeed, I remember as well," Major Lewis said with a firm nod.

"He never complained," said a woman I believed to be Mrs. Newton. I recognized her from the night of the party when Mr. Finch had died. "He always had a smile on his face."

"Mischievous, though it was," Lady Fitzwilliam said with a smirk.

That drew even further laughter.

"See? Surely, there are happy memories we have of him," Major Lewis said.

And so there were. For the next half an hour, guests shared progressively more amusing and detailed stories, to the point where I saw Mr. Newton wiping his eyes with his handkerchief and Lady Fitzwilliam waving her paper fan in front of her face, unable to control herself.

Even Mrs. Montford seemed to have found a smile or two to give, though it was difficult to see from the angle where I stood. I had noticed, however, that she had not shared a story of her own.

"Well, I am so pleased that we have all had this chance, aren't you?" the Major asked.

Nods rippled all up and down the table in response. "Yes, yes..."

Everyone else lifted their glasses, awaiting his toast, spirits newly lifted.

This was generous of the Major, I thought. *More friends should host such a heartwarming affair as a means of honoring the lives of their loved ones. Perhaps then, death would not be so—*

"And I must congratulate Mrs. Montford most of all, for being a wonderful actress," Major Lewis said unexpectedly. "She performed admirably, did she not? One might have truly believed that she grieved for our fallen friend."

My stomach dropped. What could he possibly mean?

An unsettling hush fell over the group. One by one, I watched their warm smiles falter and their curious eyes snap toward Mrs. Montford.

Major Lewis raised a single brow, his smile growing, but I detected something different there...something that sent the knots in my stomach twisting.

"Yes," he continued. "Beatrice has done a fine job of hiding the fact that Mr. Finch knew her secret and took it to his grave."

13

The silence was so utterly complete that my heartbeat sounded thunderous in my own ears.

"What secret?"

I looked around and it took me a moment to realize that the question had been voiced by Mrs. Townson.

Major Lewis's eyes darted toward Mrs. Montford in a flash.

"I speak of her secret love affair...with Captain Sinclair," he said.

Captain Sinclair. I recognized the name.

At once, I thought of the party at Lady Fitzwilliam's home. Mrs. Montford had spent a great deal of time that evening with a gentleman who, in demeanor, reminded me a great deal of the Colonel but was a bit older and with a thick white moustache.

Mrs. Montford had spent much of that evening laughing and carrying on. I remembered how pleased I had been to see her so happy. It had been some time.

My heart began to race. *Could this be true?*

It certainly could be. The night that the Colonel had died, Mrs. Montford had admitted to me that she had never truly loved the Colonel. At least, she had never been romantically in love with him. She appreciated the comfort of him, the familiarity, the consistency, and his friendship. She had not, however, loved him in a heart-wrenching, world-bending, fairytale sort of love.

That being true, was it possible that she had been in love with someone else?

All of the guests sat in stunned, uncomfortable silence, looking as if they would rather be anywhere than where they were at the moment, caught between the icy looks the Major and Mrs. Montford were exchanging.

Major Lewis, still standing at the head of the table, twirled the stem of his drink between his thumb and forefinger, seemingly oblivious to the awkwardness that had descended over the rest of the party.

Meanwhile, Mrs. Montford's body had gone as rigid as the chair she sat upon.

Mr. Jerome was the first to break the silence. "Major, I do not believe you have any right to make such an accusation against a lady in my family, certainly not in public and against a woman so recently bereaved. As a gentleman, I demand you apologize to my aunt."

Before the Major could respond, Mrs. Montford herself spoke up.

"No, Jerome, do not silence him," she said sharply. "Now that this has been brought up, despite how inappropriate the time and place, I want to answer the accusation."

She glared down the table at the Major, who studied her.

"I wish to be very clear on this subject," she said, her voice steely. "Was there at one time an especially close friendship between myself and Captain Sinclair? Yes, that much is true. However, nothing inappropriate ever occurred. Some years ago, Mr. Finch walked in on the Captain and I as the Captain was comforting me over some distressing matter. Misconstruing what he saw, Mr. Finch believed he had caught us in a compromising situation and threatened to tell my husband and others of it. I begged him not to ruin my reputation in such a way, telling him how terribly that would hurt not only the Colonel but also the Captain. I did not want to damage their friendship."

It was difficult to tell from the Major's expression whether he believed anything she had said. "Gone on," he prompted.

It was obvious she was going to continue the story, with or without his permission.

"Mr. Finch did not believe in my innocence," she recalled. "But he told me he would keep our 'secret' if I agreed to make sure that the Colonel would purchase some of his goods to sell to military friends that he was still connected with."

"Blackmail?" Mrs. Townson asked. "How...terrible."

I realized every face around the table was now watching the exchange with fascination, as though observing a drama played out on stage.

Mrs. Montford was as stationary as a doll and almost as lifeless. Her anger seemed to have evaporated now, weariness taking over. "When I kept my end of the bargain, it seemed that Mr. Finch dropped the issue entirely. I was able to move on and I made sure that Captain Sinclair and I were never alone together again after that. I knew that his feelings for me went beyond friendship, he had told me so once, and I could not risk encouraging him or feeding gossip in suspicious minds like that of Mr. Finch."

Mrs. Townson was right, I thought. Blackmail was indeed the word.

For all the good qualities his friends have boasted of in him, it seems Mr. Finch was not above betraying his friends when there was a possibility of profit.

"I have...been quite afraid of this," Mrs. Montford continued. "I knew that as soon as he was found dead, this difficult part of our history would come to light, and as such, I would prove to be a likely suspect in his murder." She gestured toward the Major, as if offering proof. "Even my oldest friends now question my motives."

It all started to make sense. Her nervous behavior, her dismissal of the man's death, her snapping at me and feigning illness to get out of speaking about it...

She is not responsible for his death. She simply did not want to be caught talking about it in the first place.

"I did not kill him, in case that needs to be stated," she said, shaking her head. "Though I can certainly see why some might think I did."

"Nonsense," her nephew said, finally speaking up again. "The Colonel is gone now. You would have no fear of Mr. Finch sharing what happened all those years ago. Who would he tell? Who would it affect, apart from yourself? No, I cannot possibly think you capable of violence."

He frowned down the table at the Major. "What is more, now that you have explained yourself, I cannot imagine any of your friends would think so little of you, either."

Murmurs of agreement swept over the table. The uneasiness seemed to be lifting.

"I can certainly understand why you were worried," Mrs. Townson said to her sister-in-law. "But the Captain is a dear friend of all our family and he has been nothing short of a gentleman all these years. He and my brother were so close, as you know."

"Yes, they were," Mrs. Montford said. "Which is why I wanted to make sure that whatever lies might be said of me, they did not ruin their relationship for the rest of their lives."

"I did not realize that Mr. Finch would take advantage of his friends in such a way," Mr. Jerome said. "It was outrageous behavior, on his part."

"As I said, he never mentioned it again after the Colonel heartily agreed to purchase some of his slings for a few of his friends when they retired," Mrs. Montford said. "I never broached the subject again, either. Mr. Finch treated me as if nothing strange had happened but, every time I looked at him, I found it difficult to forgive him."

Mr. Jerome turned to look at Major Lewis. "Major, how is it that you knew of any of this?" he asked. "It seems to me, from her explanation, that no one apart from she and Mr. Finch knew."

Major Lewis stiffened slightly. "I...Mr. Finch confided it in me some time ago."

"Why did you feel that you needed to bring it up today?" Mr. Newton asked.

Major Lewis tugged at the lapel of his coat. "Well, now you all know," he said. "To be perfectly frank, Bea, I thought it best to do this as a means of clearing the air."

Mrs. Montford stared up at him. "Clear the air?" she asked. "Why?"

"So as to ensure that no one would suspect you of the murder," he said. "Although I did not realize Mr. Finch's story about you was false, I worried it could harm you. I feared, as you have, that your secret would be discovered. I thought it best for you to admit it now, in front of so many witnesses, instead of having to admit it first to the police."

Mr. Jerome glanced sidelong at his aunt.

"I suppose there is some sense to that," Lady Fitzwilliam said. "Oh, Bea, you poor dear. How could any of us think that you were responsible for his death?"

Mrs. Newton nodded in agreement. "Yes, dear, it never even crossed our minds."

Mrs. Montford, however, seemed too defeated to hear their words of encouragement.

"You should have told us from the beginning," Mrs. Townson said. "You ought to have told the police that night."

"Why would she?" Mr. Jerome asked. "It has nothing to do with his death."

"Yes, well, it might have saved her a great deal of heartache," Mrs. Townson said.

I felt a pair of eyes on me and glanced up to see Mr. Jerome looking right at me.

His eyes were narrowed slightly, his mouth a thin, firm line.

He is suspicious, I realized. *Of me? Why?*

No, it was not of me. Someone else.

But who?

I looked just past him, over his shoulder, at the Major, who stood there watching the guests encourage and soothe Mrs. Montford.

A sneer tugged at the corner of the Major's lips and I could have sworn that I saw a dangerous glint in his gaze.

The knots in my stomach returned and I gulped.

What did he have to hide? Why did I have the sudden feeling that his plan, whatever it might have originally been, had backfired?

14

Mr. Jerome cleared his throat, drawing my attention back to him. He jutted his chin toward the door, though the motion was so subtle I wondered if I had seen it at all. He did not make me question it long, though, as he slipped his hand into his pocket and withdrew a silver pocket watch. He did not open it but he revealed three fingers to me before slipping it back in place.

Three? Minutes? Seconds?

I took a look at the ornate clock over the fireplace and found the second hand ticking by.

I waited, my eyes fixed to the moments passing by.

When three minutes had gone, I made my way from the room, slipping out unnoticed.

Outside the door, I leaned against the wall, letting out a long sigh.

I had a great many questions about everything I had witnessed in the dining room but they had to be set aside as someone else came out.

"Mr. Jerome," I greeted him.

"Good, you understood," he said. "Come with me."

We quickly made our way down the hall to a small room at the end. It was a sunroom, much like Mrs. Montford's, but nearly empty apart from a few mismatched pieces of furniture.

"I must admit that I am suddenly suspicious of our friend the Major," Mr. Jerome said.

"I am likewise worried," I said. "It seems to me that his plan was foiled by her admission. It was almost as if he said what he did as a means of...trapping her. As if he was accusing her of the murder."

"I thought the same," he said.

A nervous moment passed between us.

"It got me wondering," he said. "I wonder about whether or not he was trying to pin it on my aunt as a means of deflecting attention from himself."

"But if he is responsible, why would he have everyone here for dinner? Would he not want to avoid anyone suggesting it was him, and as you said, drawing attention to himself?" I asked.

"If I were him, I would want to do everything I could to cover my guilt," he said. "And what better way than to invite everyone here, to begin setting things up against my aunt? It is a good cover, after all, and would certainly help him to appear innocent. 'Look this way instead of at me,' as it were..."

"I suppose you are right," I said. "But we cannot act against him without evidence."

"Too true," he said, his brow furrowing. He puffed out his cheeks and air whistled between his lips.

"What is the matter?" I asked. "Are you feeling all right?"

"No, actually," he said, running his fingers through his thick, auburn hair. "I have always liked and trusted the Major. This possibility is deeply unsettling. But how can I think otherwise? The way he went after my aunt in there, it is entirely out of character for him."

"I thought I saw something sinister in his gaze when everyone else was so focused on Mrs. Montford," I said. "I did not want to see it, of course, but it felt... like a deep hatred."

"Hatred?" he repeated, his eyes narrowing. "The Major?"

I shuddered. "I could have very well been wrong, of course, worried about Mrs. Montford as I was."

"No," Mr. Jerome said, shaking his head. "You have good instincts. You have proven so time and again since we have met. I trust you, and to be honest, I feel the same."

He glanced over his shoulder, back toward the dining room.

"No one will believe us unless we find proof," he

murmured. "Perhaps no one will miss us if we do a little digging of our own?"

"What if someone catches us?" I asked, barely above a whisper.

"We must tread carefully..." he said. "But don't worry. I have a plan. Stay close."

He grabbed my hand, and together, we slipped out of the sunroom, heading for the stairs. It was where I would have chosen to go, as well, as Mrs. Montford kept her most personal and valuable belongings in the upper floors of the home where guests rarely ventured.

"Perhaps in a study or a library," I whispered as we reached the landing.

"We must—" Mr. Jerome said and stopped as he yanked me around the corner.

My heart raced as we were suddenly bathed in the darkness.

Footsteps scurried past, heading quickly down the stairs. I only caught sight of a slender shadow which came and went in the blink of an eye.

"...stay out of sight," Mr. Jerome murmured.

He gestured with a tilt of his head up the hall. I allowed him to take me along as we put some distance between ourselves and the stairs.

"In here," I whispered, tugging on his hand as we hurried by an open doorway. Deep within the blackness, I noticed the polished wooden frame of a large desk, as well as a pair of books stacked neatly atop it.

"Good find, Anna," he said, pausing to peer inside.

"Now..." he said. "I do not even know what to begin to look for. We have nothing to go on."

"Well," I said. "It would certainly have to do with Mr. Finch. What do you know of their connection?"

Mr. Jerome folded his arms, his expression difficult to see in the dark. "Not a great deal," he said. "Both men have long been friends of my mother, of course, and my late father. I have known the pair of them through my parents, and as such, I must admit that I did not pay a great deal of attention to how everyone knew one another."

I pursed my lips. "Mr. Ronald, a shopkeeper in town, told me that Mr. Finch's greatest concern was for money." I frowned. "I suppose that makes a great deal of sense, after hearing how he blackmailed Mrs. Mont-ford the way he did."

I caught sight of Mr. Jerome's profile as he peered out into the hallway. "Yes, I can certainly see why she would be worried that Mr. Finch's death could have been traced back to her, given what he had been holding over her. Well, come along, then. We mustn't waste any time. It won't be long before someone comes to look for us."

He was right. We started in the obvious places in the room, combing through the shelves and atop the bureau in the corner.

After finding nothing, we began to search the desk.

Mr. Jerome pulled the top right drawer while I searched the lower, deeper drawers.

"Strange..." he said.

"What is it?" I asked, my heart flipping within my chest.

As I straightened, I saw a pistol clutched in his hand.

"I am not surprised that he owns one, as my father had several like it," Mr. Jerome whispered. "However, this one is loaded...as if he expected trouble."

"You do not suppose we are in any danger, do you?" I asked uneasily.

"It certainly seems likely," Mr. Jerome replied. "We might as well remain vigilant."

I returned to the drawer I had been searching and was disheartened to find a great number of black bundles of paper and empty bottles of ink and fountain pens scattered throughout.

Mr. Jerome let out a sound of triumph. "Ah-ha!"

"What have you found?" I asked.

"You are not going to believe me," he said. "This and the pistol *must* have some connection to one another."

We leaned into a small ribbon of light coming into the study from the open door to the hallway.

"It appears to be some sort of contract," I said, my eyes passing over the words on the page as quickly as I could, taking in every three or four words. My eyes widened. "*...hereby agree to provide rifle slings and guards, to be presented to a one Mr. Shaw on the eighteenth of August, for the payment of...*'"

I looked up at Mr. Jerome, startled.

He nodded. "That amount seems a bit steep, does it not?"

"Steep, indeed," I breathed. My brow furrowed. "But it is unsigned," I said, pointing at the bottom of the page.

"True," he said. "And the name that Mr. Finch was to be selling to, Mr. Shaw..."

"I do not recognize the name," I said.

"I do," he said, massaging the back of his neck. "And if memory serves, that name has some sort of association with the black market."

My stomach flipped over as we were interrupted by the sound of footsteps in the hall, the *clack, clack, clack* of heels.

The drawer beside me quickly slid closed and Mr. Jerome wrapped his arm around my waist, drawing me toward himself. Before I knew what was happening, he had taken me into his arms and gently brought his lips to mine.

The whole world stopped. I could not move. I could not think.

A startled gasp came from the door but I paid it no mind. It was not until it was followed by a string of hastened apologies, and darkness filled the room as the door was pulled closed, that I realized this kiss was not without reason.

My face burned at the realization, even as Mr. Jerome pulled away.

"I apologize," he said in a low, husky voice. "I would rather be caught kissing you in a quiet place than be caught snooping through the Major's personal affects."

I did not trust my voice to speak. I simply nodded my head and brushed a stray strand of hair from my eyes.

In that moment, it mattered little that he had kissed me in a moment of convenience. I knew that he could have done any number of things to divert the attention of the unfortunate maid that had stumbled upon us but he had chosen an option that I never would have.

Has he been thinking about that? Why else would it be his first reaction?

"We should leave," he said. He reached behind me and pulled the drawer open once more. He withdrew the unsigned contract between the Major and Mr. Finch and folded it up before tucking it away into the front pocket of his coat. "I need to get this to the police as soon as I can, before the Major sees fit to pull any more unexpected tricks."

I nodded agreement.

"Let's go," he said, crossing the room and pulling the door open.

I followed after, my eyes so fully focused on him that I very nearly missed the stocky, broad man standing at the end of the hall looking toward us.

I slowed to a stop, my heart racing, fueled by fear.

Mr. Jerome's face fell as he saw what I did.

"Major..." he said.

"Hello, lad," Major Lewis said coolly. "I wondered if I might find you here."

15

15

"We were just on our way back downstairs," Mr. Jerome said, his tone cautious.

"Do not lie to me," Major Lewis said, his voice threatening. "I am not the fool you think me."

Standing this close, I could see a vein bulging in the Major's neck as he stared across the distance to Mr. Jerome. A frightful visage, to be sure, proof that he must have been quite intimidating to his foes during his time in the army.

Mr. Jerome did not answer for a moment but I saw the back of his neck stiffen. "I suppose there is no use in hiding it," he said. "Why did you make an agreement with Mr. Finch about selling his rifle slings on the black market?"

Major Lewis's brow furrowed. "There are some

things you would not understand. Best to leave matters of business to me."

Mr. Jerome said, "I would certainly like to understand what happened at my family's home the night Finch died. Did you kill him?"

"It had to be done," Major Lewis said frankly, striding past Mr. Jerome and me, making his way to his study.

"How could you do that?" Mr. Jerome asked, aghast. "He was your friend!"

My mind jumped to the agreement and what we had read upon it.

It was as if the truth struck me upside the head. "The deal fell through..." I murmured.

Major Lewis snapped his fingers. "There we go, now. The girl's got it."

He entered his study, flicking on the light as he did.

"You killed him because of an unsigned agreement?" Mr. Jerome asked, following after him.

I lingered out in the hallway, glancing down toward the stairs. *If I go now, I might be able to make it to Mrs. Montford and the others.*

"Don't think about it," Major Lewis warned.

I looked up to see him staring at me through the doorway, his eyes murderous.

"I could kill you before you reached the landing," he added. "I *will*, if you leave me no other option."

"You—what?" Mr. Jerome asked. I could see him

struggling to reconcile the dangerous man before us with the family friend he had once respected.

"You don't expect me to let this information get out, do you? Not before we make a little deal," Major Lewis said in a rumbling voice.

Mr. Jerome gave me a sidelong look and I could see the unease in his eyes. Regret, as well.

I understood all too well.

"There is a great deal about Mr. Finch that you did not know," Major Lewis informed us, sliding open the drawer to his desk. As he began to search through its contents, my heart skipped. Was that not where we had found the agreement in the first place, the agreement that was neatly tucked away inside Mr. Jerome's front pocket of his coat? "A great deal that everyone would not take so kindly to know."

"How so?" Mr. Jerome asked. He looked at me once again before darting his eyes toward the drawer. It seemed he had the same thought I did.

"It is rather difficult to make money after one retires," Major Lewis said, pulling old letters and papers from the desk, digging deeper and deeper. "That being the case, I had to find a means of supplementing my income. I found my way into some circles that many might have found unsavory, but it was necessary."

"So you lost no sleep knowing that you were doing business with criminals?" Mr. Jerome asked.

Major Lewis shrugged, seeming distracted. "Where is the blasted..." He sighed in frustration. "There was more money to be made there than helping the army directly. And wipe that indignant look off your face, boy. If you knew some of the arrangements that the military made, you would realize that what I was doing was not entirely out of—"

"I always thought you to be a man of honor and integrity," Mr. Jerome interrupted. "I admired you for it."

Major Lewis shook his head. "Lad, you would think a great deal less of me if you knew the things that I had to do in order to save my own hide during the war."

Mr. Jerome shifted uncomfortably beside me.

"Where is..." Major Lewis said.

He stopped and slowly looked over at Mr. Jerome. "You have it, don't you? That contract. Give it back to me."

Before Mr. Jerome could answer, the Major moved so quickly that I barely saw it.

He lunged across the distance between them and grabbed onto the front of Mr. Jerome's shirt. The full force of the assault caused the both of them to topple over onto the floor. Mr. Jerome collided with the floor heavily, partway out of the door into the hallway.

"Jerome!" I shouted and moved toward the pair of them, unthinking. I grabbed the back of the Major's arm and tried to pull him off of Mr. Jerome.

Major Lewis thrashed out with his arm and the force threw me backwards.

I stumbled and tried to grab onto the side of the door frame but my ankle caught on the lip of the rug. I fell flat onto my back out in the hallway.

When I rolled over to get to my feet, the Major snarled, stomping out into the hall after me.

I scrambled away on my hands and knees, trying to get away, knowing that if I turned my back for a moment—

"Anna! Look out!"

Without thinking, I threw myself aside, wrapping my arms around my head.

An extraordinary *bang!* echoed through the hall, reverberating against the walls, making my teeth chatter.

I lifted my head at the same time that a terrible, agonized scream pierced through the ringing in my ears.

I whirled around and saw Mr. Jerome standing just outside the study, the pistol clasped tightly in his hands, smoking.

Major Lewis had fallen to the ground, grabbing at the back of his leg where ruby colored blood spurted from between his fingers and splattered against the floor.

"No!" Major Lewis cried out, trying to get to his feet, reaching out toward me with bloody fingers.

The gun went off again but this time it pierced the carpet at the Major's side.

"Not...another...inch..." Mr. Jerome said, coming to stand between him and me.

A thunder of footsteps echoed from the stairwell. It was only a few moments before I heard gasps and shouts from behind us.

The other guests coming to our aid, trying to see what had happened, mattered little to me, because my gaze was squarely fixed on Mr. Jerome—and his on me.

16

"It is terribly difficult to believe that an entire week has passed since the Major was arrested," Mrs. Montford said from behind her dressing screen.

It was early in the evening. She had enjoyed her dinner an hour or so before she typically did, purely out of exhaustion from the past week's activities. Even though the Major had been arrested the night of his dinner party—as quickly as the guests were able to summon the police—the authorities still wished to speak with every guest that had been there. Mrs. Montford had been more than willing to share the same story with them that she had with the rest of us that night but the authorities had little interest in her. All they wanted to know about was the Major's business associations with Mr. Finch.

The contract that Mr. Jerome and I had found proved to be incredibly valuable. It ensured they had answers when the Major, after receiving the medical care he needed, refused to provide any.

"Well, at least we can finally put these matters behind us, what with that last letter being sent off to the authorities with my written testimony," Mrs. Montford said. "And I must admit, I do feel better, all things considered. Of course, I am grieved by the Major's actions and by the death of Mr. Finch. But a secret that I had carried for so long no longer weighs upon me and I feel a great deal freer than I have in some time."

Freedom.

It was funny, I thought, the way secrets could leave us feeling trapped in a prison of our own making. I was glad that Mrs. Montford, at least, need no longer be troubled by the shadows of her past.

I RETIRED EARLY THAT EVENING, still feeling rather exhausted since the events at Major Lewis's house.

Dreams met me almost as soon as sleep swept over me.

Darkness fell. Water lapped up against the shore. The moon glowed from behind a distant cloud, filling the sky with a dim light.

A familiar deck, with the familiar river...

I walked forward, my heart racing in my chest.

I knew it was only a moment before the shadowed figures would appear in the water and the terrible sound of my father drowning would soon fill my ears.

The struggle took place and one man shoved the other beneath the water.

I could not look away.

When the worst of the splashing stopped, the other shadow started back toward the shore, leaving my father's body behind.

However...something changed.

More splashing arose some distance away and a head appeared in the dark water, silhouetted by the moonlight. The figure it belonged to swam toward the opposite shore and climbed out.

My heart quickened. One man crawled from the river near to me...and a second left the water on the far side?

Could that be my father?

No...he was killed...

Wasn't he?

The shadow on the far shore disappeared into the night, swallowed by darkness.

When I awoke the next morning, the dream seemed distant and fantastical. Surely it was nothing more than a desire of my heart. It was too good to be true, wasn't it?

I stood at the window, staring out over the city, the same city that had haunted me for years.

Was it possible that my father was not drowned as I had always thought? Was it possible that my memory of his death had somehow been wrong?

I needed to know. I must know.

And there was only one way that I was ever going to find the truth...

Continue the mysterious adventures of Anna Fairweather with "An Unhappy Murder: An Anna Fairweather Murder Mystery, Book 5."

ABOUT THE AUTHOR

Blythe Baker is the lead writer behind several popular historical and paranormal mystery series. When Blythe isn't buried under clues, suspects, and motives, she's acting as chauffeur to her children and head groomer to her household of beloved pets. She enjoys walking her dog, lounging in her backyard hammock, and fiddling with graphic design. She also likes binge-watching mystery shows on TV.

To learn more about Blythe, visit her website and sign up for her newsletter at www.blythebaker.com

Made in the USA
Coppell, TX
03 October 2021